HADRIAN

HARLOWE SAVAGE

Monarchs
of
EROS
HARLOWE SAVAGE

THANK YOU

This is for everyone who loves a happy ending. May Persephone and Demeter bless and look kindly upon you!

Harlowe

Chapter One

"Emperor, Sir."

Hadrian put down his quill and let out a sigh. "Yes, soldier?"

"Sorry to disturb you, Sir." Hadrian turned around and shook his head, waving away the man's concern.

"What is it?"

"We've just received news from our scouts in the east, they report that Parthia is currently in the process of making war preparations."

Hadrian rubbed his temple. "When did they get back?"

"Just an hour ago." The soldier replied. "I know that we are still in the process of quelling the rebellion here, but the generals believe that the situation in Parthia requires immediate action as well as a lighter touch. They are suggesting that you head east with a majority of the army and leave behind a small contingent to finish handling the rebels here."

"Yes, I understand." Hadrian stood, completely abandoning the parchment he was working on and walking over to the soldier at the front of his tent. "Tell the generals that we will leave first thing in the morning, but let General Cicero know that he will be in charge of managing the rebellion. Then, when everything is under control here, he will meet us in Parthia."

"Yes, Sir." Hadrian did not know the name of this specific soldier, but then again, he didn't know the names of many of the soldiers in his army. He'd been Emperor for six years now and he was already bone tired of the tediousness of it all.

"You may go." Hadrian nodded and waved his hand, turning back to his desk. He didn't need to watch to know that the man had gone; growing up under the watchful eye of Emperor Trajan, Hadrian had been accustomed to rule since he was very young.

Now, at 47, Hadrian had gained enough experience and confidence over the years to know that his men respected him; but being the Emperor was exhausting.

When he finally took over the throne in 117, he quickly realized that being a stationary figurehead in Rome was not going to work for him. He wanted to see the world, travel, meet people, and exist as a person outside of the moniker of 'The Emperor.'

Carefully, he put away his quill and roll of parchment, rolling it up and securing it in his satchel. It wasn't as though he had been working on anything of incredible importance anyway. Besides, if they were going to leave first thing in the morning, he needed his rest.

Meandering over to his bed, Hadrian removed the outer layers of his clothing and hung them on a chair. He climbed into bed and snuffed out the candle, letting the darkness swaddle him like a blanket.

Typically, he liked to spend his evenings outside, gazing at the stars and consulting his astrology book, or at his desk, writing poetry until he started to get tired at around an hour or so past midnight. Even if he wouldn't fall asleep for quite some time, he could still rest and encourage his body to take the extra hours of sleep that he was offering.

It was nights like this that he hated the most. Ones where he had to just lay in his bed and stare at the ceiling until sleep finally took him. It was often nights like this that he would start to feel the sting of loneliness that had plagued him for most of his life. He was surrounded by people all the time, but there were rarely any times at all when he felt like he truly was not alone.

Perhaps he would be able to find a companion in Parthia once he'd handled the diplomatic reasons he was heading there. It didn't make things much better long term, not really. He knew that. But having a companion for a night often did the trick to stave off his desperate need for physical affection. At least for a little while.

Closing his eyes, Hadrian focused on emptying his mind. He listened to the movement of men around the campsite, the night guards chatting around the campfire and men meandering back to their tents, no doubt having heard the news about leaving first thing in the morning.

He allowed his body to still and focused on letting his limbs become heavy. Even if he didn't fall asleep right away, after years of practice he knew how to let his body get the most out of the rest that he could give it.

He let his consciousness follow each little sound that bubbled up through the night as far as it could go and then shift quickly to the next most prominent thing without allowing himself to stick with one too long. Slowly, he felt himself drifting off. Unsure of how long it had been, he just followed the feeling.

Then, a loud laugh from the campfire outside broke through the calm that he had carefully curated.

Hadrian sighed and shifted in his bed, it was going to be a long night.

Hadrian managed to get a couple hours of sleep in before one of the servants came to wake him up. As far as sleepless nights went, it hadn't been too bad. That said, he wasn't particularly looking forward to his interaction with the Parthian King.

He himself had never interacted directly with Osroes II before, but from what he had heard through his council of advisors, the man was fairly full of himself. Case in point - preparing for war out of the blue, completely unprompted.

If it truly came down to it, Rome could take Parthia in a fight, that wasn't the issue. The problem lay in the principle of the matter; he simply wasn't interested in more war. He'd seen plenty of war during Trajan's rule and was tired of it.

Rome was large enough; there was no need for more expansion, and if he could prevent another war from breaking out by traveling to Parthia and chatting with the brat calling himself "King of Kings," then that was what he would do.

As they made their way towards Parthia, Hadrian rode in silence among his generals in the front of the line. He knew the stories about him that circulated amongst the men; how could he not? That he was a stone-hearted general, unapproachable, and as professional as emperors come. In reality, he probably would have enjoyed a friendly conversation here and there, but the looming mystery around his reputation had kept his armies and generals in line for years and he wasn't one to mess with a good thing.

Parthia was out of their way, considering that had they left directly from Rome and headed in that direction, it would have been a significantly shorter journey. Now, coming up from Mauritania, they were effectively circling back toward where they had originally come from.

Needless to say by the time they reached Parthia, Hadrian was more than just a little tired.

"Are you sure you don't need to go lie down for a little while, Sire?" Felix, one of the generals who'd accompanied him on the trip, followed a couple of steps behind after they'd dropped their horses off in the stables.

"I'm fine, Felix." Hadrian retorted, not pausing in his direct path towards the palace. The sooner he got this over with, the sooner he could sleep. Preferably in a bed and not one of the cots they brought along on their journeys.

Taking that as his cue to quietly fall in line with the emperor, Felix just nodded and followed. Some of the servants helped clear the way and announce his arrival so that by the time they got to the throne room, Osroes would know he was being paid a visit by the Roman Emperor.

With about as much smugness as Hadrian expected, Osroes welcomed them into the chamber, sitting on his throne, greeting on his lips.

"Emperor Hadrian." Osroes grinned, looking down at Hadrian and his entourage from his throne. "What a pleasant surprise."

"Is it?" Hadrian quipped, crossing his arms. "A surprise, I mean."

"Well, yes. I mean, I did hear that you were headed in this direction." Osroes shrugged as nonchalantly as he could.

"Good, you must have a welcome meal prepared then. As I know Trajan welcomed you and your father when you came to visit."

Hadrian watched as Osroes' face twitched slightly in annoyance before regaining his mask of composure. "But of course. This way please. We can talk over drinks."

Osroes waved in the direction of the dining room as if dismissing them, but Hadrian stood his ground.

"Great. Shall we?"

Osroes clenched his jaw, forcing a smile. "Yes." Slowly, he got up out of the throne and walked down the steps, meeting Hadrian at ground level. Satisfied, Hadrian nodded and started towards the dining area.

Once they were seated, Hadrian took a sip from his goblet and folded his hands in front of his chest on the table.

"So, King of Kings." Hadrian mused, looking over at the Parthian King. "What's this I hear about you preparing for war?"

Osroes choked on the wine he was drinking and, after waving away a couple of servants, he put the goblet down in front of him. "Straight to the point as always I see, Hadrian."

"I find it's easier than beating around the bush." Hadrian leaned back in his chair, waiting for the other man's response.

"We are not preparing for war." Osroes smoothed a napkin over his lap. "We are simply doing some routine drills with a majority of our forces."

"That close to the border?" Hadrian prompted, unbothered by Osroes' avoidance.

"Well." Osroes pursed his lips. "There is simply more space out there, is all. I'm sure you understand."

"Of course, of course." Hadrian replied, taking another sip of his drink. "A word of advice perhaps. Be more careful about where you conduct your drills, lest someone misunderstand and attack your capital while those troops are away."

Osroes' face paled a little, clearly understanding the underlying threat in Hadrian's voice. He was incredibly irritating and far too focused on pomp and circumstance, but Osroes wasn't an idiot.

"No, we wouldn't," Osroes replied, shifting in his chair. "General."

"Yes, Sir." One of the men standing to the side stepped forward at attention.

"Call back the troops." Osroes ordered without once breaking gazes with Hadrian. "I'm sure they've had enough practice by now."

The officer nodded and swiftly exited the room.

"Excellent." Hadrian smiled softly. "Now perhaps, we can eat in peace and enjoy each other's company."

"Yes." Osroes finally broke gazes with Hadrian and focused on his food. Anyone untrained in politics might have looked in at this time to see two leaders having a meal together and engaging in friendly conversation. But Hadrian, having studied enough politicians in his day, could see the tenseness in Osroes' shoulders, the strain in his smile, and the concern in his eyes.

He looked like a kid who had just been caught stealing from the kitchen, and Hadrian was the one who busted him.

Hadrian retreated to the chambers that Osroes offered them for the night and finally let a breath out, sagging his shoulders a little and rubbing the back of his neck. Being the Emperor truly was a string of never ending problems to be solved. He remembered Trajan talking about it with him and his advisors once he'd been old enough to be included, but he didn't think that he really had a full appreciation for what he meant until after taking the throne.

Hadrian made his way over to the balcony and took a seat on the terrace, looking out at the stars. Perhaps he would get better sleep tonight, in a bed, fully exhausted from travel and playing politician all day.

Pulled from his thoughts by the sound of a door opening and closing, Hadrian turned to see a young man enter his chambers, holding a large vase. Not having noticed him yet, Hadrian watched as the young man watered the plants in his room and started to make his way around the space towards the terrace.

He seemed to be lost in his own thoughts and hadn't thought to look around the room first to see if it was empty. Hadrian found the corner of his mouth turning up in amusement. He wondered how long it would take the other man to realize that he wasn't alone. Perhaps he would miss Hadrian completely and leave the room none the wiser.

Until then, however, Hadrian was content to sit and watch the young man do his work. He couldn't have been older than 18 and his dark locks hung far enough into his eyes that Hadrian wondered if it obstructed his vision.

After about five or so minutes, the man made his way out to the terrace, poured water into one of the potted plants and then turned around, coming face to face with Hadrian. He jumped slightly, his grip slipping on the jug of water.

Instinctively, Hadrian reached out and steadied the jug so it wouldn't come crashing to the floor. Just barely, their fingers brushed as the young man readjusted his grip on the vase, Hadrian swallowed, pulling his hand back.

"I'm so sorry," the young man began, "I didn't realize anyone was in here."

Hadrian shrugged. "It's alright. I didn't really announce my presence, did I?"

The young man made a strange face for a moment before settling back on the calm demeanor he had been wearing while watering the plants. "I suppose not."

Hadrian shrugged, leaning back into his chair and gazed up to the sky. "Please don't let me distract you from doing your job."

Quietly, the young man meandered over to the other plants on the terrace, making sure to give them each enough water before placing the jug down at his feet. After a few moments of silence, Hadrian glanced over and saw that the young man was staring up at the sky as well.

"Do you ever wonder if the stars can truly tell us our fate?" Hadrian watched as the young man spoke into the space around them, not to anyone in particular.

"Sometimes," Hadrian replied truthfully. He turned his gaze away from the young man and back to the heavens. "I was told that I was born under a constellation that was indicative of great leadership and success."

"Do you not feel as though that is true?" The man prompted.

"I don't know." Hadrian crossed his arms. "I wonder sometimes. But the unfortunate bit about depending on the stars for answers lies in the fact that they cannot answer clarifying questions. It is rather annoying at times."

There wasn't an immediate response and for a moment Hadrian wondered if the man had left. But then Hadrian turned his head to the sound of soft laughter. The man was chuckling under his breath, no longer looking at the sky, but rather looking at him.

"I have never thought about it that way." The man grinned and for a moment, Hadrian was taken by just how beautiful he was. "I suppose you're right, relying solely on the interpretations of the stars can be frustrating, especially when they are vague. You know, my mother was told that I was born under the constellation that granted men great insight."

Hadrian remained quiet, waiting for the man to continue.

"Gods know what that even means. I wouldn't consider myself to be particularly insightful, but then again I do find myself wondering why everyone around me is so stupid sometimes."

Hadrian couldn't help it, he barked out a laugh and then embarrassed, he turned his head back to the sky.

"Yes, well." Hadrian felt himself smiling. "I suppose if we weren't destined for great things, we wouldn't have the wherewithal to question what we're told by those around us. My father once told me that to be truly great, one must be able to see through what people say and directly into their hearts."

The younger man made a small noise of acknowledgement.

"I'm not sure I've ever been as masterful at that as he was, but I do try." Hadrian wasn't sure why he felt so compelled to keep talking, but it was a nice feeling. "Though sometimes I find myself questioning if I am truly doing everything I can to live up to what people expect of me."

"I think we all do in a way," the man replied. "Well, I should be going. But it was lovely talking to you."

Hadrian turned his head and smiled. "Yes, I hope we will get the opportunity again."

"Me too." The young man smiled back and picked up the jug, heading towards the door.

"Wait." Hadrian turned slightly in his chair. "What's your name?"

The young man stopped and turned back around with one hand on the door handle. "Antinous," he replied before opening the door and stepping out.

"Antinous." Hadrian said to himself.

Instinctively he touched his fingers where their hands had brushed and smiled to himself. Something about the conversation had put him at ease and suddenly he was feeling tired.

Moving from the terrace to the bed, Hadrian snuffed out the lights and climbed under the covers. As he felt sleep take him, he closed his eyes and hoped that he would dream, since he rarely did. And, if he hoped that he would dream of a young man with wavy hair and beautiful eyes, nobody would ever need to know.

CHAPTER TWO

Waking to the sound of a knock on the door, Hadrian rolled over and touched his feet down to the marble floor. As he threw on his robe, he briefly noted how well rested he felt. Opening the door, he was greeted by Felix.

"Good morning, Sire." Felix bowed and gestured inside. "May I?"

"Yes of course." Hadrian nodded, stepping back so that Felix could make his way inside.

"King Osroes wanted me to convey that he has a parting gift for us, as he's sure that we will want to be on our way soon."

"Of course he did." Hadrian rubbed his face. "Well, where are we headed next?"

"That's what I wanted to talk to you about." Felix reached into his robe and pulled out a scroll, unrolling it a couple inches. "I know that we were going to continue South but since we've rerouted, there was recently an earthquake in a nearby province. Since I assume you won't want to return to Rome for the winter, I suggest that we spend some time there and help them rebuild."

Hadrian nodded and crossed his arms. "Which providence?"

"Nicomedia, Sire."

"I see." Hadrian replied. "Well, gather the troops and let them know that we will be heading to Nicomedia shortly. I will get ready to go and see whatever this 'farewell gift' Osroes has prepared for us."

"Yes Sire." Felix replied, placing the scroll back into his robes and heading toward the door.

Once Hadrian had gotten dressed and the servants of the palace had taken his bags back to the horses, he made his way down to the throne room. There, waiting for him on his throne, was Osroes.

"Ah, Emperor Hadrian. I trust you slept well." Osroes called to him with a falsely sweet voice, so uncomfortable, Hadrian was glad to be rid of the man just to never have to hear that tone of voice directed at him again.

"Yes of course," Hadrian replied cordially. "Your hospitality has been greatly appreciated, however I'm afraid we must take our leave now."

"Oh, is that so? And I had so hoped to host you here for a couple more days," Osroes replied.

Liar, Hadrian thought to himself.

"I'm afraid so," Hadrian continued in his best diplomatic tone. "Unfortunately, there was an earthquake in Nicomedia and we must leave post haste to help them rebuild."

Osroes' face twisted in what was clearly an attempt at a smile, but some of his true feelings shone through at the end.

"How honorable." Osroes shook his head and gestured to the side. "Well, I wanted to send you off with a gesture of goodwill, since you were so helpful in helping me see the error of my ways."

Hadrian glanced to the side, in the direction Osroes was gesturing and watched as ten servants walked into the throne room.

He almost considered having them sent directly to Rome to be trained in the palace, but then he caught a glimpse of a black-haired man among them, standing between two of the older women.

Swallowing and directing his gaze away from the servants, Hadrian turned back to Osroes. "Thank you. You are very generous. I'm sure that these servants will be very helpful in our travels."

He could feel Felix's surprised look on the back of his head but made no move to explain himself to the general.

"Great." Osroes smiled, folding his hands together in his lap. "I'll have them sent to your caravan so you can leave immediately. Wouldn't want to keep the earthquake victims waiting would we?"

"Of course not." Hadrian wanted to suggest that they could all walk out together, as he was interested in speaking to Antinous again, but decided he didn't want to show his hand. Osroes had clearly presented him with this gift as a burden since they were traveling. While Hadrian was not confident that the other King would take it back, he didn't want to risk it.

He watched in his periphery as the group of servants were led out the side door and into the courtyard, then he turned and took his leave out the front gate.

"I know that we are trying to maintain positive relations here, but you really didn't have to accept the servants into the caravan. We could have just had them sent directly to Rome," Felix said under his breath as they made their way down the front steps of the palace.

Hadrian shrugged. "We might need more hands to care for the earthquake victims when we get there."

Felix pursed his lips in a way that told Hadrian he was aware that ten servants wouldn't make a great deal of a difference in the grand scheme of things, but thankfully he didn't say anything about it.

In truth, Hadrian wasn't quite sure why he'd made the decision he did. He just knew that he wanted to talk to Antinous again and for one moment in his life, he decided to be selfish.

Once they arrived at the caravan, Hadrian allowed himself to look around the group to see if he could spot the black-haired man again, but to no success. They had probably been taken to one of the supply wagons which traveled further back than Hadrian would ever have an excuse to go without looking suspicious. So instead, he mounted his horse and started off in the direction of Nicomedia.

The journey was about as uneventful as any that Hadrian could remember. Now that Osroes had withdrawn his troops from the border, word had clearly spread that Hadrian and his army were in the vicinity and had reached some sort of agreement with Parthia. Consequently, they were completely unbothered as they made their way to Nicomedia.

As per usual, his tent was set up by the time he finished speaking with local authorities and creating a plan. It was just starting to get dark by the time Hadrian made his way back to his tent.

He rubbed his eyes and sat down at the edge of his bed. His body ached from the days of travel but he knew from years and years of experience that laying down now would do nothing but make him feel like there were more important things he could be doing.

So instead, he stood back up and made his way over to the desk in the corner of the tent. Since he wasn't going to be able to sleep for a while, he might as well catch up on some administrative work that had suffered while he'd been on the road.

He probably didn't need to be doing all of this on his own. Trajan used to pawn off a great deal of the administrative tasks to other high ranking officials in the palace, but something about the repetitive nature of paperwork helped put his mind at ease. It was almost meditative in a way and it wasn't like he was going to bed anytime soon.

Settling into his chair, Hadrian took a breath and started his work.

It was unclear how much time had passed since he'd sat down, but if the stiffness of his back and general lack of noises outside of his tent were any indication, it was probably late.

Unfortunately, sleep seemed to evade him just as much as it had earlier in the evening. Standing and pushing away from the desk, Hadrian made his way outside of the tent and into the cool night air.

Confirming his suspicions about the hour, most people had gone to sleep and the only other souls awake were the night guards doing their rotations.

Hadrian meandered to the center of the camp where a fire was still burning and took a seat on a log. Glancing up at the sky, Hadrian tried to recall as many constellations as he possibly could from memory. Over the years, he had gotten really good at fighting off the loneliness that often sunk in at night when everyone had gone to sleep. The trick was to keep his mind busy, because while he was wracking his brain trying to remember all the different constellations, he had no time to think about the things he was losing sleep over.

He was about fifteen constellations in when he heard a familiar voice.

"Do you always just sit outside and stare at the sky or do I just have uncanny timing?"

Hadrian looked over to see Antinous approaching the campfire.

"Well, there really isn't much to do at night other than look at the stars, is there?"

Antinous snorted and sat down on the log next to Hadrian.

"Well, I find that most people sleep," Antinous replied in a playful tone. "Though, I have heard rumors about other activities, but of course I wouldn't know anything about that."

"Of course." Hadrian felt a smile playing at the corner of his mouth. "This is an awful lot of criticism coming from someone who also seems to be not sleeping."

"Me?" Antinous pulled a hand to his chest. "Questioning the Emperor of Rome? I would never."

"Hmm," Hadrian vocalized, turning his attention back to the sky.

They sat in silence for a while, just looking up to the heavens and listening to the popping of the campfire in front of them. Almost ten minutes passed before Hadrian realized that he wasn't counting constellations anymore, he was simply content to stay sitting here with Antinous.

"You know." Antinous broke the silence, pulling Hadrian's attention back. "I would never presume to know what it's like to be Emperor, but I imagine that if you bother losing sleep over it, you're probably doing something right."

"What makes you say that?"

"Well," Antinous continued, "I know that there are plenty of leaders who make choices every day that affect millions of people and then go right to bed without a second thought about the people whose lives they just changed. For better or for worse, you know?"

"What makes you think that's why I can't sleep?" That was one of the reasons that Hadrian stayed up at night, but he was curious how Antinous had come to that conclusion.

Antinous shrugged. "You just seem like that type of person. It's like, I saw how you handled King Osroes and I'm sure that many men far more experienced in dealing with unruly children would have put him in his place, but you didn't."

Hadrian shook his head. "He can go on thinking that he's the greatest thing to ever exist. I know that he's an idiot, but intentionally provoking him would result in nothing but a war that we don't want or need."

"That's exactly what I'm talking about," Antinous interjected. "By handling him the way that you did, you put the needs of the empire and its people before your own ego. I don't know many powerful men who would do that."

"Then you must have not met many good, powerful men." Hadrian chuckled. "I was lucky enough to observe some of them in action growing up and I just try to follow in their footsteps the best I can every day."

Hadrian wasn't sure why, but he felt the need to keep sharing. Maybe it was because this was the first time in a long time, someone had treated him like a person instead of just the emperor.

"I wasn't born into royalty, you know." Hadrian glanced over to the black-haired man. Antinous said nothing, just watching Hadrian, prompting him to continue. "Emperor Trajan took me in after my parents died. I was probably about ten."

Antinous nodded. "You still think about them."

"Of course I do," Hadrian continued. "Sometimes when I'm making choices about policy or things that will greatly affect the general population, I think about my parents and how this would have directly affected them. It helps me see things from a perspective outside the palace walls."

"I think that is what makes a truly great leader," Antinous said, looking up at the stars. "Being able to consider overarching effects of their decisions and not just whether or not it will get them what they want."

Hadrian shrugged and started searching the sky again for some of the constellations he knew. "Sometimes I wonder what people will remember when they think of me generations from now." Despite these thoughts running through his head almost every day, this was the first time he'd ever said them aloud.

"I know that I won't be praised for pausing the expansion of the Roman empire. The conversations around me among the advisors and nobility tell me that much. For such a long time, Rome has been synonymous with expansion and empire. But I think it's unnecessary to expand just for the sake of expansion.

If I were off crusading for more land right now, I wouldn't be able to help the people here who need me." Hadrian paused for a moment.

"What's the point of expanding if you can't even take care of the people you're already responsible for?"

He shifted slightly in his seat. "Sometimes, I just sit and wonder if people will remember me when I'm gone. If they'll look back and say, 'He was a good man.'"

Hadrian took a deep breath and let it out, taking a moment to listen to the crackling of the fire and sit in what he'd just admitted.

When he looked over, he almost expected Antinous to be gone since he'd been so quiet. But there he was, sitting on the log and looking into the flames pensively.

CHAPTER THREE

Antinous had been right about the amount of work that needed to be done, and while Hadrian was primarily responsible for coordinating the efforts and discussing next steps with the local leaders, it was still an arduous day.

The earthquake had been devastating and the hospital had been one of the buildings to cave in, so there wasn't an ideal place for the doctors to tend to the wounded. One of the first things that they'd coordinated was the relocation of the injured to the city hall. Once that had been completed, there was the matter of salvaging as many medical supplies from the rubble as they possibly could. Then, when that was still inevitably not enough, Hadrian sent one of his scouting units to a town about a half day's journey away to gather more supplies.

Before he knew it, it was already time for dinner and he was sitting down at a table with the local leaders and his generals. They'd offered to cook something more befitting of an emperor, but Hadrian had refused. It made more sense to use those ingredients to feed more of the people who needed it.

Some of his generals had rolled their eyes, but the locals wouldn't stop bowing and thanking him for his kindness.

He had been hoping to finish up with his duties earlier in the evening so he could have a chance to look for Antinous, but unfortunately, he'd been invited to stay after dinner.

So, after everything finally calmed down, Hadrian made his way back to camp with some of the other higher ranking generals who'd stayed as well. It was fairly quiet, but there were still enough people milling around that the silence of the night hadn't yet taken over. Before he could think about it, Hadrian made his way over to the campfire that he'd sat with Antinous at the night before.

A brief scan of the area told him that his companion was nowhere to be found. Suddenly, he felt a little silly.

Just because they happened to both be awake last night and ran into each other, did not mean that the same was going to happen tonight. Besides, what if Antinous had only been humoring him and didn't have any intention of seeking him out or trying to talk to him again?

Hadrian sighed and pursed his lips.

This was ridiculous. He was almost fifty years old and here he was, sneaking around his own campsite trying to find someone that he'd just met less than a week ago.

Of course, he could use his power as the emperor to call Antinous to his side, but a selfish part of him deep down wanted to know that he had enjoyed the companionship as well.

As he was turning to leave, a soft voice stopped him in his tracks. "Looking for me?"

Hadrian felt his cheeks heat up and he slowly turned around only to see the very same person he had been agonizing about seconds earlier. Antinous looked almost amused, leaning up against a nearby cart.

"No." Hadrian lied. "I just happen to like this particular campfire."

He crossed his arms and turned his attention back to the flames and the group of soldiers sitting around it, laughing and talking about the day.

He felt Antinous' approach more than he saw it. One moment, he felt the younger man's eyes on him from behind and the next, he felt his warmth standing at his side.

"Do you ever want to sit down and join them?" Antinous' question caught him off guard and for a moment he didn't know what to say. He could just say no and avoid the awkward conversation that was sure to follow, but he didn't want to brush him off.

"Yes. Sometimes." Hadrian shrugged, watching the group of men tease one of their comrades relentlessly before finally giving him his mug.

"Why don't you?"

"This is time for them to relax and unwind," Hadrian replied, still watching the group. "They can't hardly do that when their commander is standing around, looking over their shoulders, so to speak, can they?"

Antinous hummed. "More insight from your peasant days?"

Hadrian chuckled, the sound started out low, like a rumble in his chest and eventually bubbled up to an actual laugh. "Mmm, something like that."

Finally, he gave in and looked over to Antinous; immediately he felt his heart rate pick up. The young man was grinning at him like someone might look at a friend or acquaintance.

Antinous was bold. He was treating Hadrian like they were equals, giving him a hard time, and joking along with him. He liked that.

"You don't seem to have that reservation," Hadrian noted, looking down at the shorter man. "Technically, I'm your commander too."

Antinous shrugged playfully and clasped his hands together in front of him. "I did just meet you. Give it a couple of weeks, maybe it will sink in then."

"I'd rather you didn't let it." The words slipped out of Hadrian's mouth before he could think twice. He could see the surprise cross Antinous' face but decided to commit since he'd already shown too much of his hand. "I rather like your company."

Antinous' gaze softened and he looked away, a small smile playing at his lips. "Well, that's good because I think we've had too many in-depth conversations at this point for me to just start seeing you as the emperor now."

Hadrian felt something in his chest loosen that he hadn't known was tight to begin with.

"Besides, I quite enjoy your company as well," Antinous finished, still looking off into the distance.

"Antinous!" Both men turned at the call of Antinous' name just in time to see a smaller woman, likely one of the ones that had been gifted to them by Osroes, run up. When she got close enough, Hadrian watched her go through about ten emotions at once before finally settling on a deep bow.

"Ah, Emperor Hadrian. I'm so sorry, I didn't realize."

Antinous laughed softly. "You know, from this angle, it almost looks like you're bowing to me too, Delilah."

Delilah looked up indignantly at Antinous out of what seemed to be habit, but upon making eye contact with Hadrian again, she blushed and lowered her gaze once more.

"It's alright," Hadrian prompted, "You may stand up."

Delilah cautiously lifted herself from her bow and pursed her lips.

"I was sent to retrieve Antinous. He has been reassigned to the kitchens."

"I see." Hadrian shifted his weight. He had been hoping to spend more time with Antinous but if he was needed elsewhere...

Then it hit him. He was the emperor and he could reassign Antinous to his personal entourage. Surely that wouldn't be too much of an overstep since Antinous had just told him how much he enjoyed his company as well.

"Actually, you can let your supervisor know that I've requested him for a personal project of mine and he will be reporting directly to me for the foreseeable future."

Delilah's eyes widened a little but she quickly nodded. "Yes, of course. I will let them know." Bowing once more, Delilah shot Antinous one more questioning look and then took her leave.

"A personal project, huh?" Hadrian looked over and was met with Antinous' sly grin. "I wasn't aware that we had one of those."

Hadrian shrugged, trying to ignore the way his face was heating up. "Keeping me company counts, I suppose."

"Well." Antinous clasped his hands. "I'm honored to have been chosen then."

Hadrian sighed and turned to walk towards his tent. As he moved through camp he heard Antinous chuckling behind him as they walked.

What had he just gotten himself into?

The next few days were fairly uneventful; they would wake up, make their way over to the town hall, coordinate rebuilding efforts, and discuss potential future avenues for the area's reintegration into the economy once they had enough resources to dedicate.

It felt mostly the same as his standard day as an emperor, except for one major change. Antinous was everywhere now. He was standing outside Hadrian's tent when he woke up, accompanied him to meetings, and spent time with him in the evenings when he couldn't sleep; reading or talking under the stars.

It was great, except for the small detail that he couldn't keep his eyes off of the other man. He'd known since he was a teenager that he was attracted to men, but when he'd married his wife, he tried to push that side of him back down to perform the husbandly duty he was expected to.

For the most part, it wasn't a problem. He was far too busy for wandering eyes, and his wife seemed about as equally fond of him as he was of her, so they didn't actually see each other much. However, with Antinous in his space so often, he was beginning to find it difficult to subvert his urges like he normally did.

The man could bend over in front of him and it would have Hadrian thinking such dirty thoughts that his face would break out in a full blush. The first day, he thought that maybe extended exposure would calm everything down, but it just ended up doing the exact opposite. The last two nights, immediately after Antinous had left for his tent, Hadrian had reached between his legs and stroked himself desperately to completion.

Of course, he felt a little guilty about using Antinous as an object of sexual fantasy, but he couldn't really help it.

Tonight especially, Antinous was going to kill him.

Hadrian was sitting at his desk, working on approving some reports when Antinous had decided to get some stretching in. Immediately, Hadrian's mouth went dry and it took all his concentration to keep the pen in his hand as he watched with his peripheries.

Frankly, if he didn't know any better, he would think that Antinous was doing this on purpose. He bent forward with his back to the emperor and spread his legs, alternating between one leg and the other. Then, he sat down on the floor and spread his legs impossibly wide, pressing his torso forward.

Hadrian didn't know when it happened, but he had turned his head completely and was watching with rapt attention as he felt his cock fill.

How much longer it went on for, he didn't know but before too long, Antinous lifted his gaze and Hadrian knew he'd been caught. He swallowed and cleared his throat, turning his head back down to the paperwork.

"I knew it."

Hadrian froze. He heard rustling to his side as Antinous got up off the ground and walked over until he was standing behind him.

Hadrian kept his gaze trained on the desk in front of him, not truly seeing the things in his field of vision, but instead overly aware of Antinous' presence behind him and the heavy pressure between his legs.

"Why didn't you just tell me?" Antinous whispered in Hadrian's ear, sending a shiver down his spine.

"Tell you what?" Hadrian asked, his voice raspy.

"Oh, come on Your Highness." Antinous switched ears, letting his lips brush the shell of Hadrian's ear. "You think I wouldn't have noticed?"

Before Hadrian could respond, he felt the weight of Antinous' hands on his shoulders. It was tentative, as if giving him an opportunity to clear up any miscommunication, but when he received no resistance, Hadrian felt Antinous lean his chest into his back and trail one of his hands down his chest.

"I know you think I'm attractive," Antinous murmured, his hand dipping down towards Hadrian's lap. "I've seen you watching me."

Hadrian opened his mouth to refute the claim but just at that moment, Antinous' hand brushed over his hard length and his breath hitched.

"It's okay," Antinous cooed, "I think you're attractive too."

Hadrian swallowed back a moan as Antinous palmed his cock through his pants.

"You know," Antinous continued, pulling back for a moment before taking Hadrian's hand and guiding him up out of his chair. "I could help you with that."

Antinous walked over to the cot, pulling Hadrian along and sitting him on the bed before dropping down to his knees.

Finding his voice again, Hadrian caught Antinous' hand before he could reach for him again. "You don't have to."

"I know that." Antinous smiled and gently moved his hand out of Hadrian's grasp. "But what if I want to?"

Hadrian's breath hitched again as Antinous leaned forward and mouthed him through his clothes. He shuddered as Antinous ran his hands up and down his thighs.

"May I?" Hadrian pulled himself back down from the stratosphere for long enough to look back down at Antinous. He was asking permission like he couldn't tell how badly he wanted it already.

"I..." Hadrian stuttered. "Yes."

Antinous smiled and pulled aside Hadrian's clothes, freeing his cock. Then, as if he knew exactly what Hadrian had been imagining in his nightly fantasies of him, he bit his lip and leaned forward, taking it in his hand before running his tongue from base to tip.

"Oh, fuck." Hadrian cursed. He almost looked away, it felt too real, like something out of his wet dreams come to life. But on the off chance that Antinous never wanted to do this again, he knew that he needed to take in every second. Chest heaving and eyes hooded, Hadrian watched enraptured as Antinous took the tip into his mouth and swirled his tongue around.

Hadrian leaned back onto his hands, letting his hips twitch up a little. He needed to keep his hands under control because the need he had to entangle his fingers in that dark, curly hair was nearly overwhelming.

Then, as if sensing his need, Antinous began to take more and more of him into his mouth, until his nose was buried in the curls at his base. Hadrian wasn't huge, but he wasn't small by any means either and he couldn't pretend like it wasn't the sexiest thing in the world that Antinous just took him down to the base just like that.

Hadrian groaned, his fingers twitching on the bed.

Then, just when he thought it couldn't get any better, Antinous looked up at him and swallowed.

It had been so long since he'd been intimate with anyone like this and his self control was nearly shot, so when he felt his balls drawing up, he tried to warn the other man.

"Antinous... I- I'm c..." Was all he could get out before he tipped over the edge, emptying his load down the other man's throat. "Ah... mmmm."

Antinous kept sucking him through his orgasm and only when Hadrian relaxed, completely boneless on the bed, did he pull off, wiping his mouth and shooting the emperor his signature smile.

"Same time tomorrow?" Antinous quipped lightly before exiting the tent in a hurry, leaving Hadrian alone with his thoughts.

That had been a considerably more satisfying orgasm than he'd ever been able to achieve on his own, but he still wondered in the back of his mind why Antinous had left so quickly. Fortunately, he was so spent that he was able to push that thought away and fall asleep at a reasonable time for the first time in gods know how long.

Chapter Four

Any sort of concern that Hadrian had the night before that their new nighttime activities would change the relationship they'd built thus far was put to rest the next morning when Antinous was waiting for him outside his tent as usual.

If he hadn't woken up in nearly the same position he'd been in when Antinous left, he would have been convinced that it had been some elaborate dream.

When he discussed the restoration efforts with the other generals and local government that day, they decided that they would stick around to help for another week or so before moving on. Hadrian had received an invitation from an official in Anatolia to participate in a local boar hunt and then he wanted to head down to Greece to participate in the Eleusinian Mysteries.

As much as Hadrian appreciated the hospitality of the people, he was ready to move on. There were plenty of other people in his empire that could use his assistance.

Much to do.

When he got back to the camp that night, he didn't quite feel like heading straight back to his tent, so instead he made his way over to an empty campfire and took a seat. Every now and then, Hadrian would get these melancholy feelings that would overtake him. He wasn't sure where they came from or when they would hit, but he knew that he just had to wait them out and they would eventually go away.

He closed his eyes and focused on his breathing. It got overwhelming sometimes, the loneliness. Trajan had once told him that such was the curse of the emperor, always steady for his subjects, standing strong, alone.

"There you are." Antinous' voice cut through the fog like a light shining in the dark. Hadrian turned and followed the other man's figure as he made his way over, sitting down next to him on the log. "I turned around and you were gone."

"Sorry," Hadrian mumbled, "I just needed some... space from all those people."

"Oh," Antinous remarked. "Do you want me to leave?"

"No." Hadrian shook his head. Having Antinous here was helping bring him back to the present. "Just... there were too many people back there."

Antinous made a small noise of acknowledgment and sat quietly next to him listening to the crackling of the campfire.

"Sometimes..." Hadrian continued, "Sometimes, I just wonder what my life would have been like if Trajan hadn't taken me in."

He could feel Antinous watching him, listening.

"Not that I'm not grateful," he said quickly. "It's just a lot sometimes and it can be incredibly isolating."

"There's nothing more isolating than feeling alone in a crowd."

Hadrian looked over, surprised at Antinous' comment. "Exactly."

Shaking his head, Hadrian looked up at the sky, watching the stars.

"I had a sister."

Hadrian glanced over to Antinous at his admission but upon seeing the other man's gaze toward the sky as well, he looked away.

"What happened?"

"She was a sickly kid," Antinous continued, "Always needing the healer, trying every medication under the sun, but none of it did any good. Everyone was always so focused on her that it was hard not to feel like a burden."

Hadrian wanted to reach over, take Antinous' hand, and tell him that he wasn't a burden, but he got the sense that wasn't what he needed right now.

"I was always surrounded by people, my parents, my sister, doctors, neighbors, everyone always coming in to check on her and make things better, but nothing ever worked.

I always tried to spend as much time with her as I could, but I felt like I was in the way. Despite all of that, I could tell that she was happier when I was around. I was the only person who didn't treat her like she was sick.

We played and talked about stupid things that didn't matter. I still don't know if I should have been sneaking in to hang out with her when my parents told me that she needed to rest, but…" Antinous paused and let out a puff of air.

"I think she knew that she wasn't going to get better and I think I knew that too. To tell you the truth, everyone probably did, but they wouldn't admit it. I just wanted to spend as much time with her and give her as much joy as I could before her time was up.

She died when I was 11 and my dad shortly after that; he never really got over it. So, I started working at the palace under Osroes to bring in some extra money. It worked out for a while, but then my mom got sick and passed away too. At that point, there wasn't really anywhere else for me to go except the palace, so I stayed."

Hadrian turned his head and looked over at Antinous this time to find him looking back.

"I'm not saying that I can presume what it feels like to be an emperor or to know what the loneliness at the top feels like, but I just know… I know what it's like to feel alone in a crowded room."

Hadrian looked back and forth between the other man's eyes, searching for any sense of pity, but finding none.

"I'm sorry about your sister," Hadrian managed.

Antinous nodded. "Thanks."

"Trajan was the closest thing I had to family after my parents died." He had no idea why it was so easy to talk to this man, but with each word they exchanged, it was like the weight in his chest got lighter little by little. "I never had any siblings so I never got to experience anything like that.

When Trajan took me in, the loneliness that was born out of my parents' untimely deaths was lessened little by little. I was always so afraid that something would happen and that I'd be alone again, so when Trajan suggested that I marry his niece, I thought, 'what a great idea.'" Hadrian scoffed, looking down into the campfire.

"Not such a great idea, I assume?" Antinous prompted, a hint of amusement back in his voice.

"Let's just say," Hadrian continued, "We don't exactly get along."

"Is she truly horrible?" Antinous asked.

"No." Hadrian shook his head and leaned back slightly on his hands. "She's not horrible. We just aren't very compatible for a variety of reasons.

So, when I became emperor, I decided to travel around, partly so that she could have her own life outside of me and partially because I don't think I could stand to look at her everyday and know that-" Hadrian stopped short, the words caught in his throat.

He half expected Antinous to prompt him again, but when he didn't, Hadrian took a moment to regain his composure.

"I couldn't stand to look at her everyday and know that I'd fallen short of the vision Trajan had wanted for me."

"I'm sure he would understand," Antinous murmured. Hadrian almost didn't catch it over the sound of the campfire but he did.

"I don't know." Hadrian shrugged. "I just try to follow in his footsteps in every other aspect of my rule to try and make up for it."

As he sat, watching the fire, Antinous next to him, he couldn't help but feel a little less lonely that night.

The rest of the week went by quicker than Hadrian had anticipated. Adding a deadline to all the things that needed to be done set a fire under everyone, not only to complete what they were tasked with doing, but also in preparation to leave.

He saw Antinous a couple of other times intermittently, but the night they'd sat around the campfire talking, they'd been interrupted by Felix.

Felix was wondering if he could borrow Antinous for one of the rebuilding endeavors. Given the new deadline, they were a little short on manpower and could use everyone they could get. Not wanting to deny the people what they needed, Hadrian had acquiesced, if not a little begrudgingly.

He found that he felt better when Antinous was around, so by the end of the week, he was in what could very easily be described as "a mood."

As they ate dinner on their last night at the camp, Felix made a comment that made Hadrian realize that he wasn't as subtle as he would have hoped.

"Don't worry." Felix said between bites. "I will give Antinous back to you first thing in the morning before we set out."

Hadrian was so taken aback that he'd been made that he had no response. It was all he could do to keep chewing and not choke on his food. He could have sworn that he saw Felix smile slightly from his peripheral vision at his non response, but he couldn't be sure.

"Thank you." Hadrian replied.

He'd been alone for so long that he'd almost forgotten what it was like to have consistent companionship. So when it had suddenly been taken away from him again, he must have shown more of his hand than he'd meant to.

It was bad enough that he missed the other man, but the fact that other people were noticing was a whole other level of strange.

They were...

What?

Friends?

Hadrian thought back to that night in his tent when Antinous had gone down on him and then immediately left and felt himself heat up.

Lovers?

No. They hadn't done anything since and besides, he wasn't using Antinous for sex. He knew that other emperors and high ranking officials sometimes took lovers outside of their marriages, but he'd always been on the move far too long for anything consistent. Sometimes he would visit the odd brothel during their travels when the urge hit him particularly hard, but no one that he would ever consider referring to as a lover.

Or even a friend for that matter.

Hadrian scowled down at his food.

It would be good to get back on the road. Staying in one place for this long was starting to mess with his head.

"I'm going to retire for the evening," Hadrian said to Felix as he stood from the table. He nodded to the other officials and thanked his hosts for the meal before making his way to the door.

Hadrian walked back to the camp in silence. Part of him was hopeful that he'd see Antinous tonight but another part of him was afraid of how much he'd come to depend on the other man in a matter of weeks.

But, of course, since the universe had a sick sense of humor, that choice was made for him. Turning the corner, he almost ran face first into the one person he happened to be thinking of.

"Hadrian." Antinous smiled. "I thought you were still at dinner."

"I left early." Hadrian shook his head and continued towards the tent, Antinous at his side. "I enjoy the company of my generals as much as the next person, but gathering for dinner every night can be a lot."

Antinous made a small noise of approval.

"So, no more building houses?" Hadrian inquired, holding the flap to the tent open. "I haven't seen you in nearly a week."

"We just finished up," Antinous replied, his head ducked down a little, but Hadrian could still see the slight flush across his cheeks. "Why? You miss me?"

Now it was Hadrian's turn to be bashful. He looked up at the roof of the tent, avoiding eye contact.

"Maybe."

Evidently, the universe deemed now to be the perfect time for Hadrian to realize that this was the first time they'd been alone together since that night in the tent.

And if Antinous' fidgeting body language was any indicator, he'd likely just realized as well.

"Well, then it won't be too humiliating for me to tell you that I missed you, too."

Hadrian lowered his gaze to meet Antinous' eyes, only to find him looking back.

"You know, you left in quite a hurry the other night," Hadrian commented. "Of course, I would understand if you didn't want to do it again…"

"No." Antinous replied almost a little too quickly, blushing further. "That's not…"

Hadrian raised an eyebrow and waited for the younger man to continue.

Antinous huffed and darted his eyes back and forth a couple of times. "I just got a little too into it, is all."

"So, you left to - um?"

"Go handle it, yes." Antinous finished in a rush.

Hadrian couldn't help it, he felt the laugh bubbling up from deep in his chest and was utterly helpless when it reached his lips.

"Well, it's not that funny." Antinous pouted, crossing his arms.

"No, no," Hadrian got out between chuckles. "That's not it."

Hadrian stepped forward, closing the distance a little between the two of them. Now that he knew Antinous hadn't done it out of some sort of twisted sense of obligation, he felt a million times lighter.

"Just…" Hadrian reached out and placed a hand on Antinous' waist, pulling him a little closer. "Let me take care of it for you next time."

Antinous' eyes were wide with disbelief, but he uncrossed his arms and stepped further into Hadrian's space. "Really?"

"Really," Hadrian murmured, bringing his other hand up to the younger man's cheek, tilting his head up slightly.

"An emperor, catering to a servant, I wonder what the rest of the camp would say," Antinous said, doing his best to sound scandalized.

"Nothing, if they know what's good for them." Hadrian smiled as Antinous laughed. "Besides, I think you and I both know that you've never just been a servant to me."

Antinous looked up and met Hadrian's gaze. The air almost crackled with the amount of tension between them. Antinous licked his lips and leaned a little closer.

CHAPTER FIVE

They were so close, just one more inch and he could finally claim Antinous' mouth with his own.

"Emperor, sir." A voice from outside the tent rang through and Antinous jumped a little. Hadrian pulled back and turned toward the entrance, hands on his hips.

"Yes?" He said, exasperatedly.

One of the soldier's from Felix's battalion entered the space. "The general wanted me to bring you this, he said he forgot to give it to you at dinner."

The man handed Hadrian a scroll, and then stepped back.

"Is that all?" Hadrian asked.

"Yes, Sir."

"Dismissed." Hadrian waved his hand and the soldier was gone.

As he turned back around, he was greeted with a very grumpy looking Antinous.

"That was the worst timing he possibly could have had. I mean the general just saw you, couldn't it have waited until tomorrow? I mean we were clearly in the middle of someth-mmmph."

Mid-sentence, Hadrian cleared the distance between them and pulled Antinous into his arms, finally kissing him. Antinous immediately melted into his embrace, the tension from his annoyance dissipating.

Hadrian ran his fingers up through the back of Antinous' hair to get a better angle on the kiss and with his other arm, pulled the smaller man in as close to his own body as he could until there was no space between them.

Antinous made a small noise as he wrapped his own arms around Hadrian's neck, who swallowed it happily. Slowly, Hadrian walked the pair of them towards the cot. Then, when Antinous' legs hit the side, Hadrian braced one of his arms on the mattress, lowering them both down until Antinous was laying on his back, Hadrian hovering over him.

Hadrian swallowed. Antinous was truly so beautiful. His black hair looked tousled and unruly and yet impossibly soft at the same time. Reaching out, Hadrian ran his fingers through the other man's hair, leaning in to kiss his neck.

Despite his trips to brothels, Hadrian was actually quite the romantic. He liked to take care of his partner and spend the time to make them feel loved. He certainly hoped that Antinous could feel that under his touch.

As he kissed down Antinous' neck, he lowered his hips down, pressing their bodies together again. Antinous' breath hitched at the contact and he immediately ground up. Hadrian could feel the other man's cock hardening under his clothes and fuck if that didn't just go straight to his dick.

Moving back up, Hadrian claimed Antinous' mouth once again, licking in. Antinous opened his mouth eagerly and ran his own tongue over Hadrian's, giving just as good as he was getting and taking exactly what he wanted.

Cradling Antinous' face with one hand, Hadrian ground his hips tentatively down, gasping softly at the feeling of their cocks sliding against each other through the fabric. He was content to continue at that leisurely pace, but it seemed as though Antinous was not as patient. With one swift movement, Antinous flipped them so he was sitting, straddling Hadrian.

Hadrian chuckled but gave over control, moving his hand down to Antinous' hips.

"Gods," Antinous murmured between kisses. "I've been wanting to do this since you first agreed to let me suck you off. You're way too sexy."

Hadrian couldn't help the smile that came to his face as Antinous spoke, but instead of responding, he moved his other hand from the shorter man's face, down to his hips and bucked his own hips up.

Antinous gasped and grabbed Hadrian's robe with both fists, leaning over into the emperor's shoulder. "Fuck. You're gonna make me cum like this."

"That is the idea," Hadrian replied, smiling to himself. He reached his hands further back, grabbing Antinous' ass and using his leverage to slot them together even closer. The drag of Antinous' body against his own was very quickly becoming overwhelming and he could feel his orgasm building.

Antinous was not faring much better as his own rocking hips began to stutter and his breath came in desperate puffs.

Just as he was about to cum, Hadrian reached up and pulled Antinous' hair back with one hand as he whispered in his ear.

"Come for me, baby."

As if directly one cue, Antinous seized up, hips twitching as he moaned. The feeling of Antinous cumming on top of him was exactly what Hadrian needed to fall over the edge himself.

He grunted as he came, holding Antinous close. As he rode out the end of his orgasm, he wasn't sure how much time had passed, only that Antinous' lips were on his again. However, this time it wasn't fevered, it was gentle and loving.

Hadrian let himself take Antinous' face in his hands and kiss him gently like he was the most precious thing in the world; which, right now, it felt like he was.

Hadrian pulled them both up so they were on the pillow and threw the blanket over them, pulling Antinous close again.

"Damn." Antinous mumbled through kisses. "I really wanted you to fuck me."

Hadrian chuckled and brushed Antinous' hair out of his face. "Mmm, next time."

"Next time?" Antinous' face lit up a little at the promise and Hadrian felt his heart clench. So what if he was developing feelings for the other man? It was clearly mutual and he hadn't allowed himself to be so close to anyone in a long time. Didn't he also deserve good things?

"Yes. Next time." Hadrian nodded, placing a single kiss to Antinous' forehead.

Antinous buried his face in Hadrian's chest and wrapped his arms around him as well. They lay like that for a few minutes in silence before Antinous spoke up again.

"You know, I'm going to fall asleep if you keep rubbing my back like that."

"Good." Hadrian mumbled, already feeling himself drifting off as well.

"Well, I have to warn you," Antinous continued. "If I fall asleep here, I'm not going back to my own bed tonight."

In response, Hadrian just tightened his embrace and buried his face in Antinous' curly locks.

Antinous chuckled. "Well, alright then." Hadrian let himself relax into the bed as Antinous snuggled closer, accepting his fate.

Then, for the first time in gods know how many years, Hadrian fell into a peaceful sleep.

The first thing that Hadrian registered when he woke up was how rested he felt. Then, the next thing was the warmth radiating from the body next to him. They had changed positions in the night, but hadn't strayed too far away from each other. Hadrian scooted closer and pulled Antinous in close to him so that he was spooning the younger man from behind.

In his sleep, Antinous cooed happily and shuffled backwards, holding onto Hadrian's arms wrapped around him.

Hadrian smiled to himself and watched as Antinous slept soundly. It was probably right before dawn and his generals would come looking for him soon in preparation to leave, but he probably had some time to himself. Besides, he hoped that he would get many more mornings like this with Antinous.

Leaning down, Hadrian kissed the nape of Antinous' neck, covering as much skin as he could reach. Antinous sighed and pressed his hips back a little into Hadrian's crotch. Hadrian chuckled, feeling 20 years old again.

He pressed forward towards Antinous' plush ass and continued his assault on Antinous' neck while rocking steadily against the other man. Even asleep, Antinous was incredibly reactive, he moaned softly, leaning into the kisses and from his vantage point, Hadrian could see the tent already forming beneath his clothes.

Hadrian ran his hand along Antinous' side, down to his hip and squeezed. He felt himself hardening against Antinous and sent up a little thank you to the gods for feeling so well rested.

He slotted his cock between Antinous' butt cheeks and used his leverage on the other man's hip to increase the pressure. Traveling up to Antinous' ear, Hadrian nibbled at his ear lobe, this time eliciting a louder, more coherent moan, followed by his name.

"Mm, ahh Hadrian."

Hadrian felt his cock pulse as Antinous called his name and slid his hand down from his hips to his now, leaking cock. Antinous inhaled sharply as Hadrian palmed him through his pants.

"Ah... what a wonderful way to wake up," Antinous murmured.

Hadrian smiled, now that he knew that Antinous was fully awake and enjoying his participation in activities, he removed his hand and sat up slightly to pull off Antinous' pants completely.

"Mmm, are you gonna fuck me?" Antinous asked, his voice dripping with desire.

He wanted to, desperately, but they likely didn't have time and Hadrian didn't want their first time to be a quicky in a tent.

"Not this morning, baby." Hadrian whispered into Antinous ear. He remembered how much Antinous had liked that nickname the night before when they were being intimate and if he was being honest with himself, he liked the taste of the name on his tongue.

Antinous whined, almost pouting.

"But I am going to take care of you, don't worry." Hadrian reassured him with a soft chuckle. Without fully taking his own pants off, he pulled his erection out and rubbed the tip along the crack of Antinous' ass.

"Oh fuck." Antinous moaned, rocking his hips back into Hadrian.

Hadrian bit his lip and angled his cock so that he could slip it between the other man's thighs. Understanding Hadrian's intentions, Antinous opened his thighs a little to make space and then closed them again once they were settled.

Hadrian reached around to Antinous' front and took his leaking cock in one hand before beginning to thrust.

Before Antinous could make any louder noises however, Hadrian kissed him deeply, working his tongue inside and reveling in the fact that Antinous was kissing him back just as passionately.

With each drag of his cock, he could feel the bottom side of Antinous' dick, his balls, and his taint. Despite knowing how sensitive those areas were, he knew that Antinous probably wouldn't cum from that alone, so he began stroking the other man's cock in time with his own thrusts.

Despite having cum only last night, Hadrian felt himself working towards the edge already. Typically he would have to work himself for quite some time to get to this point, but Antinous was just so sexy pressed up against him, it was like his body had a mind of its own.

Hadrian kept thrusting and stroking until Antinous broke the kiss, his head falling back onto the pillow.

"Fuck… Hadrian…" Antinous's hips twitched forward with each movement. "You're gonna make me cum."

Hadrian groaned, feeling his own balls drawing up. "Cum for me baby."

Then, almost as if on command, Antinous' body tightened and he came, shooting his semen off the bed and onto the floor.

Fuck that was hot, Hadrian thought.

Antinous reached down between his own thighs and began playing with the head of Hadrian's cock. The secondary stimulation was nearly too much and Hadrian tipped over the edge almost immediately.

Hadrian bit his lip as he came, grunting with effort before finally settling back down into the bed. He let his softening cock slide out from between Antinous' thighs and took a deep, satisfied breath.

Antinous turned around and wrapped his arms around Hadrian's neck, kissing him.

"I think I could get used to this," Antinous murmured between kisses.

"Well, good because I wasn't really planning on letting you go back to sleeping alone now was I?"

Antinous pulled back a little with an incredulous look on his face, one of not quite disbelief but of surprise. Hadrian ran his fingers through Antinous' hair and the younger man leaned into the touch, closing his eyes.

"Emperor, Sire?" Hadrian rolled his eyes with exasperation as the guard he had been expecting called him from outside the tent. He and Antinous clearly had some things they needed to talk about, but right now, duty called.

Hadrian rolled out of bed and tucked his cock back into his pants. He leaned over the bed once more and pressed a kiss to Antinous' forehead.

"I'll be right back," he murmured before straightening up and walking over to the tent entrance. He stepped outside and came face to face with a very surprised guard who clearly hadn't been expecting him to come outside to meet him.

"Ah, Sire." The guard bowed, a little flustered. "I was just here to deliver the news that we are almost finished packing up camp, once we finish taking down the tents, we will be ready to depart."

"Understood." Hadrian nodded. "Thank you."

The soldier bowed again and scuttled away at the dismissal.

Hadrian breathed in the crisp morning air and ran a hand through his beard. Emperors were typically clean-shaven, but Hadrian had never really understood the appeal. It was a hassle to shave daily while on the road and the beard gave him insulation against the wind and cold when they were traveling. Besides, Antinous didn't seem to mind it.

Hadrian turned back around and reentered the tent to find that Antinous had gotten up and put his clothes back on.

"You know, you could have stayed in bed a little longer," Hadrian commented, sitting down at the desk.

"I didn't know if you were coming back right away." Antinous admitted, blushing a little. Gods, he was so cute.

"Well, it's alright." Hadrian turned his chair so that it was facing the middle of the room. "We are supposed to be leaving soon anyway."

Antinous raised his eyebrows and tentatively walked over, stepping between Hadrian's thighs. Hadrian lifted his arms and placed his hands on Antinous' hips. Antinous relaxed a little, placing his own hands on the emperor's arms. It was almost as if he wasn't sure that the affection outside of sex was going to be well received.

They definitely needed to talk.

"Where are we going?" Antinous grinned, tilting his head.

"To Greece," Hadrian replied. He enjoyed the way that Antinous' facial expressions changed ever so slightly with each response he was given. "We are going to participate in the Eleusinian Mysteries."

"Seriously?" Antinous asked. "I would never have taken you for a follower of Demeter and Persephone."

"Why am I not surprised that you know what that is?" Hadrian chuckled, running his thumb back and forth on Antinous' hip.

"Well, I don't know the details." Antinous shrugged. "I don't think anyone who hasn't participated really knows, but I've heard of it, of course. We used to have a shrine to Demeter in my childhood home; you know, to pray for a good harvest that year."

Hadrian made a small noise of acknowledgment. "Makes sense."

"It's held in Athens, is it not?" Antinous continued.

"Yes." Hadrian pursed his lips. "Unfortunately it won't just be a trip for participating in the festivities, at least for me. Recently, we got a message from the Athenian leadership requesting that I look over their constitution and work with them on resolving a couple of other things that they wouldn't give too many details about prior to our arrival."

"Well. I'll try not to be underfoot while you're trying to work." Antinous quipped, it was clearly a joke but there was something a little bit off about the way that he said it that had Hadrian holding on a little tighter to the other man's hips.

"Actually." Hadrian averted his gaze slightly. "I was hoping that you'd stick around."

Antinous perked up at this admission a little.

"I found that I was quite distracted while you were off rebuilding houses and I think that I'd be able to focus a little better if I knew you were nearby."

When Hadrian turned his gaze back to the younger man, that look of surprise and confusion was there again, but was quickly replaced with a soft smile.

"Well." Antinous said matter of factly, running a hand down Hadrian's arm. "We can't have you being all distracted now can we?"

Chapter Six

I t was strange for Hadrian to use his influence as emperor for something as selfish as keeping Antinous by his side since he didn't tend to use his power for himself. But, after announcing to Felix that Antinous was going to be riding next to him during the journey and not assigned to any specific tasks upon arrival, Felix simply nodded and said he'd inform the rest of the generals.

Throughout the entire process, Antinous remained silent, standing slightly behind Hadrian at all times until they were finally on horseback. They chatted and joked the entire ride to Athens and Hadrian watched as the tension drained from Antinous' shoulders as they fell back into their comfortable banter.

Every now and then, one of the generals would ride up to speak with him and Antinous would fall silent, pulling his horse slightly behind Hadrian's until the conversation was over. Whenever this happened, Hadrian would have to gesture for Antinous to come back up before he would rejoin him.

The more Hadrian interacted with other people with Antinous around, the more he became attuned to his companion's changes in demeanor. When other people were around, Antinous would shrink back and fall into the role of silent servant. Hadrian knew that he had been a servant but something about it rubbed him the wrong way.

When they finally arrived in Athens, they were greeted by the royal guard and escorted into the palace while the troops were shown to an area they could set up camp.

"Emperor Hadrian." A deep voice boomed through the hallways and Hadrian looked up to see Aegeus. "I'm so glad that you've made it safely."

"Great to see you as always, Aegeus." Hadrian closed the distance between them and took the other man's hand. Aegeus was a little taller than Hadrian himself and had dark, curly hair like Antinous. He had been the man who'd initially reached out to Hadrian for political assistance earlier on that month. He'd heard that the emperor had planned to come down to Athens for the Mysteries and had taken advantage of that opportunity.

"I'm sure you're exhausted from your trip," Aegeus continued, walking with them through the marble halls. "Let me show you to your rooms."

Aegeus led them through a labyrinth of columns and intricately decorated hallways. Outside, Hadrian could see the gardens that spanned across the property between individual buildings. Aegeus was talking shop about something going on with the olive oil producers and some sort of quota they were supposed to be imposing, but Hadrian was more interested in Antinous tailing behind them.

Once Aegeus had stepped up to Hadrian's side, once again, Antinous had slipped into the background, walking five steps behind them. It was distracting him to the point that somewhere in the conversation, he'd lost the train of conversation and was just making small noises of acknowledgment.

It wasn't until Aegeus stopped in front of a door, looking directly at Hadrian that he realized he'd been asked a question.

"Apologies, Aegeus. It's been a long day of travel and I'm afraid that the political conversations are going to have to wait until tomorrow," Hadrian lied, rubbing his face with one hand.

"It's quite alright, Sire." Aegeus smiled sympathetically and opened the door. "Here is where you will be staying, the Imperial Suite."

The three of them walked into the room and stopped just short of the entryway. It was clearly the nicest room in the palace, prepared ahead of time for Hadrian's visit. A huge canopy bed took up the focal point of the room and behind it were large windows looking out onto the garden.

"Will your servant be needing additional accommodations?" Aegeus asked, gesturing to Antinous.

Antinous just flicked his eyes down, avoiding eye contact with the other man and Hadrian felt anger boiling in his stomach.

"He is not my servant," Hadrian replied, jaw tight.

"Ah." Aegeus nodded and waved his hand. "Consort then."

Hadrian snapped his gaze up to Aegeus about to say something when Antinous spoke up.

"No, that's alright." Both Hadrian and Aegeus looked over at the younger man. His gaze was still to the floor, but Hadrian recognized the spirited way of speaking from their time together. That alone was the only thing to allow his anger to subside.

Deflating a little, Hadrian sighed and turned back to Aegeus. "No, that's alright, he will be staying with me."

"Understood." Aegeus quipped, seemingly unaware of the frustration running just below Hadrian's skin. "Well, again, it's so wonderful to have you here. I will send someone to get you when dinner is prepared. Make sure to get some rest. We are all very excited to have you."

With that, Aegeus took his leave, shutting the door behind him.

"I'm sorry." Antinous piped up, lifting his gaze from the floor. "I spoke out of turn, you just looked like you were about to kill him."

Hadrian ran his fingers through his hair and sighed. "No, it's alright. I'm the one who should have been more clear."

"I mean," Antinous continued shrugging. "There's not much to clarify is there?"

Hadrian watched as Antinous fiddled with his fingers, avoiding direct eye contact.

"If I'm not your servant then I am your consort. It's simple." Antinous shrugged.

Hadrian felt that uneasy feeling in the pit of his stomach return and he closed the distance between them, taking Antinous by the wrist. He led them over to the bed and sat them both down so they were facing each other.

"No. It's not," Hadrian insisted. "Is this why you've been walking behind me and acting differently around other people?"

Antinous ruffled his brows. "Yes, of course. I mean, it's all fine and good if we talk with each other like we are just friends and lovers in the comfort of our own rooms, but in front of everyone else..."

Antinous paused and shifted in his seat. "Hadrian. You are the Emperor. It's only natural that you wouldn't want other people to see how close we are. It makes sense, I get it. You don't have to worry about sparing my feelings."

"Well, what about my feelings?" Hadrian snapped. Antinous looked back at him with a look of utter confusion.

Hadrian sighed and took one of Antinous' hands in his own. He had never had to have a conversation like this before and wasn't sure where to even begin but so far their relationship had been based on honesty, so that seemed like the best way to go.

"I don't want the people closest to me to treat you like a consort or a servant. I don't like how they just disregard you whenever I come into a room, it doesn't feel right." Hadrian scratched his beard with his free hand.

"Antinous, you are the closest thing I've ever had to a true partner and I don't like that you feel the need to hide that. I got married to Vibia when I was 24 at the urging of Trajan's advisors. She was Trajan's grandniece and it just made sense especially because I hadn't been pursuing anyone else at the time.

I'd hoped that it would work out even though I very clearly preferred men, but Vibia and I didn't... don't get along. Frankly, I try to stay as far away from her as possible for as long as I can. I don't want to say that's the primary reason I travel so much, but it's definitely a contributing factor.

Gods, we've been married for over 20 years now and I can count the number of times that we've had honest conversation. We didn't even sleep in the same bed on our wedding night, needless to say she's never actually let me touch her despite the nobles urging us to produce an heir. Frankly, I don't even know if I'd be able to perform if she did let me close enough to her to try; she's kind of terrifying."

Hadrian paused and rubbed his thumb against the back of Antinous' hand.

"I've basically been alone my whole life and you're the first person who has actually taken the time to get to know me for who I am. And that means something to me, beyond just having a consort or a servant who knows my needs better than anyone. Above everything else, I like to believe that we are friends, Antinous, and I don't like it when people treat the people I care about like they're not worthy."

Hadrian watched his thumb running back and forth on Antinous' hand in an attempt to avoid whatever look he knew Antinous was giving him right now. He'd known that they needed to have this conversation, but he had been hoping that it would have been during a relaxing evening as they talked under the stars. Not after a near miss with a local dignitary.

Even so, he mustered the courage to lift his gaze and meet Antinous' eyes. Immediately he felt his heart drop as he saw tears spilling from the corners of the other man's eyes.

"Antinous... I'm sorry I-"

"No." Antinous shook his head and placed his free hand on top of Hadrian's. "Don't apologize. I'm not upset."

Hadrian closed his mouth and just watched, letting Antinous continue.

"I just didn't know you felt that way." Antinous' voice cracked. "It's not a secret that I like you. I'd hoped that after we were gifted to your army that I might get to talk with you a couple more times. But I knew I would probably need to fabricate those situations to make them happen. But then you sought me out and spent time with me of your own accord; I was so happy and I thought that just being near you would be enough."

Tears were now freely flowing down Antinous' face and Hadrian had to hold himself back from reaching up and wiping them away.

"But then I had to go and push for more. I'm the one who suggested taking things to the next level and I was terrified that you'd realize how much I liked you and send me away. But then, you asked me to stay and..."

Antinous shrugged and smiled up through his tears.

"It doesn't matter to me what other people think because as long as you want me here, that's all I could ask for."

Hadrian didn't make the conscious decision to move but before he knew it, he had fully closed the distance between the two of them and pulled Antinous into his arms.

"I wouldn't ever send you away." Hadrian said into the top of Antinous' head, chuckling. "I was worried that you were only going along with what I wanted because I'm the emperor."

Antinous shook his head in Hadrian's chest before looking up, arms winding around Hadrian's waist. "Guess we are both pretty stupid, aren't we?"

Hadrian nodded and brought one hand up to Antinous' cheek, cupping his face, and Antinous smiled, leaning into the touch. Hadrian felt his heart skip a beat as he looked down at Antinous and was overtaken by the sudden need to kiss him. In the days leading up to this moment, he would have resisted, but now he knew he didn't have to.

Hadrian leaned down, kissing Antinous gently on the lips. Antinous brought his hands up to cup his face in return, pressing up onto his toes slightly to deepen the kiss.

Hadrian wrapped an arm around the smaller man's waist and lifted him off the ground, walking them over to the bed.

"Please tell me you're going to fuck me now," Antinous whispered against Hadrian's lips with a smile.

"Mmm. Tempting," Hadrian teased, placing the black haired man gently on the bed. "But no, not yet."

Antinous whined as Hadrian kissed across his jaw and down onto his neck.

"I think," Hadrian continued, pushing Antinous' shirt up so he could press kisses to his torso. "That I just want to hold you tonight, is that okay?"

"I suppose." Antinous grinned, letting himself be pushed back down onto the bed.

Hadrian cupped Antinous's face and ran his fingers through the younger man's hair. "I just never want you to doubt that what we have is real. That I'd still want you even if we never did anything sexual at all."

Antinous raised his eyebrows in surprise, but didn't argue.

"You're not my servant, Antinous." Hadrian murmured, peppering kisses all over Antinous's face. "You're not my consort."

Hadrian couldn't do anything but smile as he pulled Antinous into his chest, the younger man snuggling in, wrapping his arms around Hadrian's waist.

"You're so much more than that."

CHAPTER SEVEN

Hadrian laid next to Antinous, running his fingers up and down the younger man's back as they cuddled. For the first time since he'd met him, Hadrian actually felt like Antinous was fully relaxed.

Antinous was almost purring with contentment as he snuggled down in Hadrian's chest. They had to meet downstairs later for dinner, but right now, Hadrian was content to spend his time here in this room, with Antinous. Honestly, he couldn't remember the last time he'd felt so happy.

Now that both of their feelings were out on the table, Hadrian didn't have to hold back when he wanted to be affectionate. It was truly incredible.

Even though he'd been married for decades now, he had never felt the way that he was beginning to feel for Antinous. Part of that was scary, but part of it was incredibly liberating and Hadrian was excited to see where all of this would take him.

Gently, he leaned in and kissed Antinous on the cheek, rousing the shorter man from his rest. Antinous stretched in Hadrian's arms and looked up, grinning sleepily.

"Hey you," Antinous murmured, placing a soft kiss to Hadrian's lips.

"Have a nice little nap?" Hadrian teased, running a hand through Antinous' curls.

"I did, thank you." Antinous grinned even larger.

Hadrian sighed. "Well, I wanted to wake you up before we had to go down for dinner."

Antinous blinked a couple of times. "I thought you were having dinner with the other nobles."

"We are." Hadrian nodded, watching as the implication sunk in.

"Hadrian." Antinous sat up. "You can't seriously be considering taking me to that dinner with you."

"I'm the emperor, I can do whatever I want," Hadrian shot back.

Antinous shook his head in exasperation. "I suppose you're right, but..."

"But nothing." Hadrian took Antinous' face in his hands. "Are you doubting my power as emperor?"

"No." Antinous laughed. "I'm not. It's just-"

Hadrian waited, looking back and forth between Antinous' eyes. "Just what, baby?"

Antinous' cheeks automatically went bright red at the pet name and Hadrian ran one hand through his dark curls.

"I know what you're thinking and I don't want you to worry about it."

"I know that we are together," Antinous continued. "But, emperors don't typically bring people who used to be their servants to big, important dinner parties."

Hadrian sighed. "I won't force you, but I know that I would feel a lot better with you by my side tonight."

Antinous covered the hand Hadrian had on his cheek with his own and took a breath. "You're too sweet, you know that?"

The shorter man shifted in his seat and bit his lip. "If you want me to go, I will. But I want you to be aware that certain people might not be the most excited about my attendance."

Hadrian nodded. He'd known that it might be a possibility, especially after the way Antinous had been acting around other people over the past few days. He also knew that he'd never seen Trajan or any other noble for that matter bring someone that wasn't their wife to an official event.

He knew that Trajan had kept a few lovers in the palace over the years, but now that he was thinking about it, he'd never really seen them interact much except for when Trajan called for them. Thinking about Antinous in that way made Hadrian's stomach uneasy and he knew that he never wanted whatever this was to be summed up in that way.

Even so, he was taking a risk bringing Antinous to the dinner tonight, but if he was going to start introducing him as his partner, he needed to start somewhere. And tonight seemed like just as good an opportunity as any other.

"I'm not worried," Hadrian replied. "If they're going to be upset, they'll be upset. I just know that I don't want you to ever question how much I care about you. On top of that, if I go without you, I'll only be thinking the entire time how much I want to leave so I can come back here and spend time with you."

Antinous giggled at that.

"At least this way, there will be a possibility of me actually getting some work done."

Antinous nodded. "Were you really that distracted the week that I was helping with the construction?"

"Absolutely," Hadrian confessed. "Even Felix noticed, which was horribly embarrassing for me. I was told that my entire mood shifted."

Antinous smiled and took Hadrian's hand in his own. "Well, we can't have that, can we? If you're distracted, certain things might slip through the cracks that you need to pay attention to. Frankly, I should be near you all the time for the sake of national security alone."

Hadrian laughed. "I'd be amenable to that."

"Alright," Antinous conceded before furrowing his brows. "Oh gods, Hadrian."

"What?"

"I have nothing to wear to a fancy dinner."

Hadrian smiled and pressed a kiss to Antinous' forehead. "I think I can probably help with that."

Antinous feigned surprise. "Are you telling me that you just so happen to carry around extra clothes that are far too small for you just in case someone needs them?"

"No." Hadrian chuckled. "But being the emperor does have a few perks."

A few hours and a couple try-on sessions later and they were both ready to go. Hadrian walked down the hallway with Antinous' arm linked in his all the way to the dining room. Aegeus and his wife were there waiting for him along with a couple other high ranking nobles that Hadrian recognized from his previous trips here.

Hadrian could see on Antinous' face that he expected someone to question his presence here, but no one said anything. Walking in on the arm of the emperor and in nice clothes nonetheless, Antinous blended in nicely.

"So I have a dispute that I need your insight on," Aegeus began from across the table.

"Is that so?" Hadrian took a sip of his wine, squeezing Antinous' knee comfortingly under the table.

"Yes." The servants put down the first course and Aegeus launched into his clearly prepared speech. "We've been having some trouble with the olive oil producers in the territory. Obviously we want to encourage commerce as best we can, but there is always going to be a price to doing said commerce in certain territories. I'm sure you know."

Hadrian made a noise of acknowledgment, taking another sip of wine. This was the one thing that he hated about visiting territories in the empire. Local authorities seemed to be under the impression that he was going to agree with them simply because they were the ones in charge; when in reality, Hadrian had a much stronger track record of siding with the common man.

"The Athenian Assembly and Council recently implemented a production quota to ensure that the oil needs across the territory are being met, and the producers are fighting back." Aegeus shrugged. "They seem to think that the quota is too steep and will cut into their bottom line."

"What's wrong with just letting them produce the amount that is being demanded?" Hadrian inquired, feeling that this wasn't the whole story.

"Well," Aegeus swallowed his bite of food. "Some of the oil needs to go to the facilitators who coordinate the trade. The quota would help the producers ensure that they would have enough left over to pay the facilitators without issue."

"Ah." Hadrian put his wine glass down. "So you would have me do... what?"

"If you wouldn't mind issuing a decree backing up the need for the quota, I'm sure that would put the oil producers minds to rest."

"Perhaps." Hadrian had to actively try not to roll his eyes. "However, issuing a decree for the entire territory might be a little too ambitious. I prefer not to utilize middlemen at all when it comes to free trade personally, but I do not proclaim to know what the exact situation is here. So, perhaps it would be better if I left the legislation in this particular instance in your capable hands."

This was a song and dance that Hadrian had done many times before. One of the things that Trajan had taught him at a young age was how to reframe ideas and concepts in a way that they might be received a little better than they would otherwise. Turning Aegeus down and praising him for his prowess as a leader in one breath would confuse and satiate him all in one go.

"Ah yes." Aegeus took a drink of wine. "Of course, thank you for your faith in me."

He was clearly disappointed that Hadrian hadn't taken his side, but frankly seemed more confused than anything else.

"How are preparations for the Mysteries coming?" One of the nobles redirected the conversation, asking Aegeus directly.

"That was very impressive." Hadrian heard Antinous whisper.

He turned his head to see the younger man looking over at him with a smirk.

Bringing his wine cup up to his lips to hide the movement of his mouth, Hadrian replied with a small smile. "When you've been doing this as long as I have, you start to get a knack for it."

Hadrian took a drink and took Antinous' hand under the table, twining their fingers together.

"How's your food?"

"It's amazing." Antinous nodded. "We used to sometimes get leftovers if we worked the kitchen the nights that Osroes would have dinner parties but having the whole plate to myself is a treat."

Hadrian's heart jumped in his chest, squeezing Antinous' hand. "Well, you'd better get used to it because you are not abandoning me at any of these parties. From now on, if I have to go, so do you."

Antinous's gaze softened and he ran a thumb over Hadrian's hand.

"I don't believe we have met before." The wife of one of the nobles who was seated next to Hadrian leaned forward and made eye contact with Antinous.

"Ah." Antinous smiled. "I don't believe we have."

The woman tilted her head, waiting for him to continue.

"I was taking up residence in Parthia until recently. I've only joined H... Emperor Hadrian this month."

"Oh interesting!" The woman smiled at them both. "My name is Helen and I am the wife of Senator Linus. We have been attending these dinners for years and this is the first time the emperor has ever brought a companion so you're obviously an individual of interest, I'm sure you understand."

Hadrian could feel his cheeks heating up a little. He'd expected people to bring attention to the fact that Antinous was there, but he hadn't expected that they would draw attention to his hermit-like habits.

"How is Vibia?" Helen continued, now directing her attention to Hadrian directly. "I have always wanted to meet her but she never seems to be with you when you visit."

Hadrian took a drink of his wine and put on his best political smile. "Oh, Vibia doesn't like leaving the capital. I'm sure that we could arrange a visit for you though, if you would want to go see her."

"Oh I couldn't possibly impose." Helen waved her hand in front of her face. "Besides, the Senator has too much to do here to possibly entertain the idea of a vacation like that."

"Well," Hadrian continued. "I suppose things like that cannot be avoided can they?"

"I suppose not." Helen smiled. It looked like she wanted to continue the conversation but thankfully, her attention was pulled back to the main conversation occurring further down the table.

On their way back to the room after dinner, Hadrian did his best to keep up his political facade as effectively as he could until he closed the door to his room. Immediately he let out a breath and ran his hands through his hair. It was only after he'd dropped his facade that he remembered he was not alone.

Turning towards Antinous, Hadrian smiled softly. "Sorry." He apologized, walking over to the bed. "Being a political figurehead is exhausting."

Antinous padded over to the bed and sat down behind Hadrian, draping his arms over the older man's shoulders. "You really don't let anyone else see you like this, do you?"

Hadrian shook his head, holding onto Antinous' hands. "No, I don't." Hadrian tightened his grip on Antinous. "If it's too much, I can try to ease the transition a little-"

"No," Antinous interrupted Hadrian's apology softly but firmly. "I know you're used to doing all of this on your own, but I like that I'm the only one who gets to see you like this."

Antinous placed a kiss on the side of Hadrian's neck. "I like that you're comfortable enough with me to show this side of you."

Another kiss.

"And I would never ask you to pretend in front of me."

Another.

"Let me be your safe place, Hadrian."

Antinous moved his hands back to Hadrian's shoulders and started kneading his thumbs into the tense muscle. Immediately, Hadrian's eyes slid closed and he sighed, leaning into the touch.

"When that door is closed, I don't want you to worry about what people think of you, what you're supposed to be doing or not. I just want you to relax and be yourself. Emperor Hadrian is impressive, absolutely, but I still like this version of you more."

Hadrian bit his lip, feeling his throat choke up a little. He could feel the wetness gathering at the corners of his eyes, but he was determined not to let them fall. So instead, he just took another deep breath and focused on the sensation of Antinous' hands on him.

He had only known Antinous for a short period of time, but it truly felt as though he'd known him for years. Hadrian had never truly been in love, but he imagined that if he had, it would feel something like this.

CHAPTER EIGHT

A fter a while of just sitting with Antinous, Hadrian finally resolved himself to get up.

"As much as I am enjoying this, we should probably bathe." Hadrian turned and looked over his shoulder at Antinous.

"Mmm," Antinous hummed. "Probably."

Hadrian got up off the bed and turned back around, extending a hand to the black haired man on the bed. Antinous smiled and took it, pulling himself up onto his knees and placing a single kiss to Hadrian's lips.

Together they made their way to the bathing chamber attached to the room and Hadrian shed his robes, looking over at Antinous as he did the same. His eyes raked over Antinous' naked form and he swallowed, feeling himself beginning to get worked up.

Padding across the tile, Hadrian walked over to Antinous and took him in his arms, hugging him from behind. Antinous dropped his head back on Hadrian's shoulder and made a soft, contented sound. Hadrian could feel himself getting harder pressing up against Antinous' backside and evidently Antinous felt it too, moving his hips slightly.

Hadrian groaned, kissing down Antinous' neck, unable to stop his hips from pressing forward. Antinous sighed and turned around taking Hadrian's mouth with his own. Hadrian could feel the younger man's hardness against his thigh and let his hand wander down to take a handful of Antinous' ass.

"Mmm." Antinous moaned. "Please."

Hadrian let his hand move further down until the tips of his fingers were playing at Antinous' hole.

"Yeah?" Hadrian asked, teasing the smaller man by rubbing small circles around his entrance but not moving inside.

"Yes, yes…" Antinous' breath began to pick up and Hadrian felt his cock twitch. "I want you so much…please."

"Have you ever?" Hadrian prompted, pressing the pad of his finger against Antinous' hole.

"Ah! Yes, I have… so, please…"

"Perfect," Hadrian murmured, kissing Antinous deeply again and letting his middle finger slide in. Antinous whimpered in pleasure as he pressed his hips back even more into the touch. Hadrian used his other arm to lift Antinous, giving him a better angle to press in even further.

Antinous was so much smaller than him that he could lift him with very little effort. So, with a quick glance, Hadrian gauged where the tub was and carried the black haired man over, taking the steps down into the water without ever pulling out.

Once in the water, Hadrian set Antinous down on one of the steps and brought his legs up over his shoulders, Antinous' head leaning back on the tile of the floor just out of the water. Tentatively, Hadrian pumped his finger a couple of times, watching in satisfaction as Antinous' face heated up and his cock twitched against his stomach.

"Oh fuck." Antinous moaned, pulling Hadrian's face down to his for another kiss. Hadrian kept pumping his finger until Antinous was writhing against him, begging for more. Only then did he nudge a second finger against the other man's entrance and slide it in slowly next to his first.

Carefully, Hadrian began scissoring his fingers to stretch Antinous out. He was larger than average and he wanted this to be good for both of them.

Antinous panted into his mouth, hips rocking back and forth, desperate for some traction on his cock, but Hadrian held back. He tactically avoided Antinous' erection and instead focused his attention on fingering the man and running his other hand up and down Antinous' body; across his thighs, over his stomach, and supporting his back.

Antinous' moans were getting louder, the sounds going directly to Hadrian's dick. He was suddenly very grateful for his insistence that they didn't do this for the first time in the tents. He wanted these sweet sounds all to himself.

"Oh, Hadrian... please, fuck me now... please..." Antinous begged through pants.

"Almost, baby." Hadrian grinned, adding a third finger. "I need to make sure you're nice and ready for me."

Antinous threw his head back and moaned loudly, doing everything he could to fuck himself down on Hadrian's fingers. However, instead of letting him, Hadrian used his other hand to hold Antinous' hip, keeping him where he was. Then, with a turn of his wrist, he felt his finger rub against a slightly raised area and Antinous gasped.

"Oh fuck…"

"Is that it?" Hadrian leaned in, touching his lips to Antinous' ear. "Is that your spot, baby?"

"Unghhh…" Antinous panted, unable to respond verbally for a moment, but instead just nodded profusely.

Hadrian stopped fully thrusting with his fingers and instead turned his attention directly to that spot, rubbing it tirelessly. Antinous gasped and moaned, writhing against Hadrian's fingers.

"Had…Hadrian- please, you have to stop… I'm gonna cum."

Hadrian chuckled low and bit at the shell of Antinous' ear. "Think you can give me two?"

"Ahh- I nggg…" Antinous seized up, cumming instantly. As his hips rose out of the water, he came onto his chest, some of it hitting the tiles behind his head. Hadrian rubbed him through it until he whined from overstimulation. Only then did Hadrian pull his fingers out and pull Antinous into his arms again in the water.

"You are a menace." Antinous sighed, laughing into Hadrian's shoulder. In one movement, he wrapped his legs around Hadrian's torso and pulled his head back so that he could look him in the eyes.

Hadrian felt his still very hard cock, poke at Antinous' ass as they moved together in the water.

"What are we going to do about that, huh?" Antinous teased, wiggling down so Hadrian's cock brushed over his ass.

"Mmm... I don't know," Hadrian said between kisses. "You mentioned something about wanting to get fucked, but I don't know what your refractory period is like."

Antinous gasped in mock offense. "You wound me."

They grinned at each other and Antinous pressed a light kiss to the tip of Hadrian's nose.

"Let's wash up and then I will show you just how quickly I bounce back, how's that?"

Hadrian grinned and nodded. "Sounds good to me."

Quickly they cleaned up, never straying too far from one another. Every now and then, Antinous would reach down and give Hadrian's cock a couple of strokes, partially to tease him the way he had been teased, he was sure. By the time they were done and had dried off as best they could, Hadrian practically booked it to the bed. He was reaching out for Antinous before laying down, but the shorter man seemed to have different plans.

Antinous shook his head and pushed Hadrian back onto the bed. Hadrian scooted up so that his head was on the pillows and his cock was standing tall. Antinous climbed up after him and before making his way fully up to lay next to Hadrian on the pillows, he stopped short, licking a stripe up Hadrian's cock.

Hadrian groaned, feeling himself begin to leak. He'd been worked up long enough that any little touch was enough at this point to get him fully going. Antinous took him fully into his mouth and bobbed his head a couple of times, lubing up Hadrian's dick with his spit. Then, with the most obscene slurping noise Hadrian had ever heard in his life, he pulled off.

Climbing up on top of Hadrian, Antinous swung his leg over Hadrian's torso and situated himself over his hips. Leaning forward, Antinous caught Hadrian's lips with his own again and began kissing him deeply as his hand reached back around and grasped Hadrian's cock. As they kissed, Antinous tilted his hips back slightly, finding his hole with Hadrian's erection and pressed the tip up against himself, pulling moans out of both of them.

Then, reluctantly relinquishing the kisses, Antinous sat up fully, before lowering himself down and impaling himself on Hadrian's cock. He did it so slowly that Hadrian had to bite his own lip and breathe to not thrust up into the warmth like he wanted to. Swallowing, he screwed his eyes shut and gripped Antinous' hips, helping direct him down.

"Don't close your eyes," Antinous whispered.

Hadrian opened them to see Antinous watching him, a fucked out glow about him as he took his dick. He could see it disappearing into the dark haired man and bit his lip even harder.

"I want you to watch me... as I take your cock," Antinous got out between panting breaths.

Had Hadrian been any younger and less experienced, he would have cum right then and there, just from the sight and Antinous' words alone. So, in that moment he thanked the gods that they hadn't met any earlier in life.

Finally, Antinous sat fully on Hadrian's lap, taking the last of it and leaning forward, propping himself up on Hadrian's chest.

"Fuck... you're huge." Antinous moaned, testing the fit as he bounced slowly up and down a couple of times.

When Antinous moved his hands off of Hadrian's chest, Hadrian felt his mouth go dry.

"Oh fuck." He cursed, reaching out and placing a hand on Antinous' lower stomach. Each time he lowered himself down, Hadrian saw his cock bulging out from his abdomen ever so slightly.

Antinous moaned, "Fuck, you're so deep."

Hadrian felt his own breath picking up as Antinous moved faster, bouncing on his lap, his own cock bouncing against his stomach with each movement. Antinous was a powerhouse, small and lean but strong as hell, he kept bouncing on Hadrian's cock non-stop until his thighs were shaking so much, he couldn't keep up the rhythm anymore.

"Hadrian... please... I can't." Antinous whimpered as his pace began to stutter.

Understanding what he was asking, Hadrian adjusted his grip on Antinous' hips and planted his feet on the bed, taking over. He thrusted up into Antinous at a punishing pace, relishing each whine and moan he pulled from the other man. Then, in a frenzy, Antinous gripped himself and started stroking furiously.

"Hadrian... I'm close- I'm gonna cum." Antinous panted, stroking his cock in time with Hadrian's thrusts.

Hadrian could feel himself teetering on the edge as well and that confession gave him permission to chase his pleasure. A couple more thrusts and suddenly Antinous was cumming, he shot cum all over Hadrian's chest and stomach and as he did, he clenched around Hadrian's cock.

That added pressure wrung Hadrian's orgasm right out of him, as he slammed up one more time, unloading inside of Antinous. He felt that orgasm right down to his toes as he humped up a couple more times, riding out the final waves before finally pulling Antinous down for a kiss.

With a sigh, Antinous rolled to the side, curling in on Hadrian, flinging one leg over the emperor's. Hadrian scooted closer, putting an arm around the shorter man and letting him rest his head on his chest.

"Was it worth the wait?" Hadrian broke the silence, running his fingers through Antinous' black curls.

Antinous barked a short laugh. "Yes, of course. I think you just fucked my brains out."

Hadrian chuckled, holding the hand Antinous had resting on his chest.

"However…" Antinous continued. "I think we are going to have to take another bath."

"That's alright," Hadrian responded, taking a deep breath. "We might as well take advantage of the amenities as long as we have them. I'm sure there will be days on the road where we won't be able to bathe."

Antinous scrunched his nose in disgust. "I know. Let us not speak of that right now."

Hadrian laughed as they sat up and meandered back over to the baths.

"Mmm, I think all those years in the palace have made you soft," Hadrian joked.

Antinous rolled his eyes, a grin spreading across his face.

"Oh come on, you love me anyway."

Hadrian watched as the gravity of what he just said sunk into Antinous' face. The shorter man froze with one foot in the water, looking back at him.

"I'm sorry, I didn't mean-"

"It's okay," Hadrian interrupted, passing him on the steps before pulling him into the water after him. "I um, think I might be getting there at least."

Antinous' face turned a bright tomato red in an instant, sinking down into the water.

"Really?" His voice was so soft that had they not been so close to each other, Hadrian would have missed it.

"Yes, really." Hadrian nodded, pulling Antinous into his chest. "I get it if you're not there, or even thinking about it. But, I wanted you to know."

Antinous' eyes widened for an instant before throwing his arms around Hadrian's shoulders and burying his face in his neck.

Hadrian chuckled, holding the smaller man in the water. He was so adorable.

"Me too," Antinous mumbled into Hadrian's neck and Hadrian felt his heart leap.

"Well, good."

"Good."

Hadrian pulled back and took Antinous' face in his hands before kissing him deeply. Antinous sighed happily, leaning into the kiss and tilting his head to deepen it.

Hadrian was content to just remain there, kissing in the water, but Antinous pulled away.

"Okay, we need to stop unless you're ready for another round." Hadrian laughed, running a hand through his beard.

"Well, we do have some things to do in the morning." Hadrian shrugged, taking Antinous' hand.

"Then we should probably rinse off and try to sleep." Antinous bit his lip, raking his eyes down Hadrian's form, pausing at his crotch below the water for a moment before shaking his head. "No. Sleep." He tore his gaze away.

Hadrian smiled, feeling his face heating up. It had been quite some time since he'd been looked at with that level of desire and the fact that it was coming from Antinous made it all the better. But Antinous was right, if they were going to be at all functional in the morning, they needed to finish up and head to sleep.

"So wise for your few years." Hadrian teased, earning himself an exasperated look from his young lover.

They washed off quickly and as soon as they were dry, they migrated to the bed in the center of the room, climbing under the covers. The space was much larger than their cot they'd been sleeping on previously, but instead of spreading out, it was almost as if they gravitated towards each other, cuddling in a tangle of limbs.

"I'm really happy you're here with me," Hadrian admitted, petting Antinous' hair in the darkness.

"Me too." Antinous whispered. "You know, I've never had a boyfriend before."

Hadrian hummed in response. "Me neither, but something tells me that we will be able to figure it out."

Antinous hugged him tightly and kissed him softly on the lips.

"Goodnight, Hadrian."

"Goodnight."

CHAPTER NINE

T he morning came far too early for Hadrian's taste given how much they had traveled the day before, but with consciousness also came with the warmth of Antinous snuggled up at his side.

Waking up like this made it worth it, he thought as he pulled Antinous in closer. The sleeping man made a small, pleased noise, settling his head on Hadrian's chest.

He was going to let Antinous sleep a little longer but a knock at the door had him sighing. Antinous shifted, waking from the sound.

"Yes? Come in," Hadrian called.

The door cracked open and a servant woman walked in, keeping her eyes to the floor.

"Your presence has been requested at breakfast, Your Majesty."

Antinous buried his face in Hadrian's neck, hiding from the morning intruder.

"Understood. We will be down shortly."

The servant bowed and backed out of the room, shutting the door behind her.

"Gods, do you always have people walking in on you when you're in bed?" Antinous grumbled, rubbing his eyes.

"Yes, it comes with the territory." Hadrian chuckled. "But now that I have a roommate, I will see what I can do about the frequency of that, what do you say?"

"I think that sounds perfect." Antinous tilted his head up, smiling sleepily at Hadrian.

The pair got up out of bed and dressed, finding their way down to the dining hall once again. Felix met them outside of the bedchamber and updated them as they went.

"Later today, the feast will be held at the temple of Demeter. Once that has been taken care of, we will participate in the Lesser Mysteries before retiring for the evening. Then, later this week, if deemed worthy, we will participate in the Greater Mysteries."

"Felix," Hadrian inquired. "You've participated in the ceremonies before, correct?"

"Yes." Felix kept his answer short and sweet. Hadrian knew that to participate in the mysteries, one had to swear a vow of secrecy. Even being invited to participate was a huge deal and the invitation was said to only be extended to the worthy. Even then, once the first set of mysteries was completed, only a select few would be approved by the priests to continue to the Greater Mysteries.

Hadrian hummed in acknowledgment. "So you'll be participating in both no matter what?"

Felix glanced to the side. "Yes. I participated in the mysteries once when I was a child. It has been quite some time since I've been back, however, so it should be an interesting experience nevertheless."

"Why are the priests so hush hush about the ceremonies?" Antinous piped up, glancing around Hadrian at Felix.

Felix frowned and twisted his mouth in thought. "I don't remember much about the actual ceremonies themselves as I was far too young, but I believe that it has to do with something received by the worthy at the ceremony."

Hadrian raised his eyebrows.

"Again, I was young so I can't remember exactly what happened but I probably wouldn't tell you even if I did. It's a crime to reveal what you've learned during the ceremonies and you can get put to death for it."

"Huh." Antinous fell back into step with Hadrian as they entered the hall. "Well, thanks for telling me what you could, I guess."

Felix nodded, stopping at the door and letting the other two continue on to the table. Hadrian had been invited to the mysteries but the invitation hadn't been only for him. It read, 'Hadrian and Guest'.

He had assumed the invitation had meant Felix since he had participated previously, but if what Felix had said was true, he would have been welcomed either way.

Regardless, he was glad to have the extra invitation so that Antinous could accompany him. Based on the way his face had lit up as Felix told them what he could about the ceremonies, he seemed to be excited and ready to go.

Breakfast passed uneventfully, typical noble conversations and obvious attempts to win his favor, but nothing truly of value. Antinous set his hand on his knee about halfway through breakfast and Hadrian relaxed a little, not knowing he'd been tensing up. He shot a thankful look at Antinous and gave his hand a little return squeeze under the table.

When he looked up however, he noticed Aegeus eyeing them suspiciously. However, before he could say anything, a herald entered the room announcing that it was time for them to move the party down to town. A festival was being held in honor of the mysteries and it would be a great way to pass the time before the feast later in the day.

The town was decorated meticulously in the colors of spring, flowers lining the streets and hanging from every doorway.

"My mom always used to put out flowers at the start of spring in honor of Persephone returning to her mother from the underworld." Antinous leaned in as they made their way down a side street.

"Really?" Hadrian remembered very little from his childhood when his parents were still alive, but from what he did remember, that seemed like something his own mother might have done.

"Yeah," Antinous continued. "She was so adamant about it that you'd think she thought that she and she alone was responsible for guiding Persephone back each year."

Antinous laughed at the recollection before a pensive, thoughtful expression came over his face.

"I didn't continue the tradition after I moved to the palace. Sometimes I wish I had."

Hadrian reached over and took Antinous' hand in his own. "Well, I suppose we will just have to get some flowers here to put out when we get back."

"Really?" The clouded look cleared from the younger man's face and Hadrian paused, running a hand through his hair. He would do anything to make Antinous happy. Anything.

"Of course."

Antinous beamed. "That would be great. Thank you Hadrian."

Just as Hadrian was about to respond, his attention was pulled by the sound of someone clearing their throat.

Glancing down the street, the pair saw Aegeus standing with some of his entourage, hands on his hips.

"I believe there is a parade about to start in the town square." Aegeus shifted his weight from one foot to another. "I thought I might fetch you so you wouldn't miss out."

"Thank you, Aegeus." Hadrian turned, Antinous' hand still in his own. "What do you say?" He asked turning to Antinous. "Shall we go see a parade?"

Antinous glanced back to Aegeus' looming form at the end of the street for a moment before turning back, giving Hadrian's hand a squeeze.

"That sounds fun," He replied.

Hadrian was glad they'd had their conversation the night before about the nature of their relationship because despite the looks he had been getting all morning, it was nice to be able to be affectionate with Antinous outside of the privacy of their room.

The group made their way to the town center together, stopping only briefly to take a look at the festival foods and wares the townspeople were offering. They were almost there when Hadrian was approached by a small group of people.

"Emperor Hadrian, Sire." The woman at the front spoke as they all bowed. "Might we have one moment of your time?"

Aegeus frowned, stepping forward. "How dare you interrupt the emperor while he attempts to enjoy the festivities. If you need to speak with him, you may do so later, on his time."

"It's alright Aegeus." Hadrian put up a hand to stop the man from encroaching any further on the group. "Give me just a moment, alright?"

Aegeus didn't look happy about it, but he nodded, gesturing to his guards.

Hadrian turned to Antinous. "Go on ahead, I'll catch up alright?"

Antinous smiled softly, rubbing his thumb across Hadrian's hand. "Alright. You're wonderful for doing this, you know."

"Oh." Hadrian felt his face heating up a little. "Hush. Just go save me a spot."

Antinous laughed lightly. "I don't think you'll have a hard time finding a seat regardless, Mr. Emperor, but sure." Antinous stood up on his toes, kissing Hadrian on the cheek before letting go of his hand and following Aegeus.

Hadrian turned to Felix. "Keep an eye on him, okay?" He asked, gesturing with his head in the direction Antinous had walked in. He wasn't sure if he was talking about Antinous or Aegeus given how aggressive he'd just gotten with the citizens, but Felix seemed to understand either way.

He nodded and followed with his hands behind his back, leaving Hadrian with a few of his other guards.

"What did you need?" Hadrian asked, turning his attention back to the woman at the front of the group.

The woman bowed her head even lower. "Thank you so much for taking the time to speak with us."

"Of course. Raise your head." Hadrian replied, feeling less stressed as the group of people stood up straight.

"Well, Athens has been experiencing a drought for quite some time now and we are having a difficult time getting enough water. We understand that you likely have a lot on your plate right now, but if it isn't too much to ask; perhaps you could help us find a solution?"

Hadrian nodded thoughtfully. "Does this city have aqueducts?"

"One," the woman replied. "But, it seems that the area it was bringing water from has dried up with the drought."

"Is there a place nearby that still has water that hasn't been tapped yet?"

"Yes, Mount Parnes still has a supply of water. In fact, that's where most of us get the majority of water we need for our basic day to day." The woman shrugged. "However, it's a rather long journey to bring water there and back all the time."

"I understand." Hadrian nodded. "If Parnes still has resources that are usable, the smart thing to do would be to build an aqueduct from there, down to the city center."

"Oh, that would be wonderful," one of the women cooed. "If another aqueduct would be possible, that would help tremendously."

Hadrian paused for a moment, crossing his arms. "Is it true that the leadership has put a quota into place for olive oil producers?"

"It is," a man in the back spoke up. "Unfortunately, that's one of the reasons for the lack of water in the first place. Normally we would put a pause on growing until the drought ended, but with the quota, most of the water we can still get from the original aqueduct has to go into growing the trees."

Hadrian felt his eyebrow twitch at the admission. He'd told himself that he wouldn't get involved but this was one of the things he hated most about politicians; they never considered the long term consequences to the choices they made. He would just have to start construction on an aqueduct as soon as possible and see if that made a difference.

"I see," he replied. "Well, thank you for letting me know. I will see to it that construction begins on another aqueduct as soon as possible."

"Bless you." The woman in the front bowed down again and the rest of the group followed suit.

"Enjoy the festivities," Hadrian said, turning back towards where his group had wandered off to. He walked for a couple of minutes before seeing the familiar silhouette of Antinous. However, as he made his way towards the group, he began to hear the words being exchanged between Antinous and Aegeus.

"It's shameful," Aegeus spat. "If you truly used to work in the palace of Osroes, you should know that servants have a place."

"I am not a servant." Antinous frowned, crossing his arms.

"Fine, concubine then." Hadrian felt his anger boiling in his stomach as Aegeus completely disregarded everything Antinous was saying and continued on. "It's none of my business who the emperor chooses to fuck in the privacy of his own room, but you should know better than to sit at the same table with us and dare to treat us as equals."

Hadrian had heard enough. With three large steps he closed the distance between them, appearing in front of a now shocked Aegeus.

"Emperor Hadrian…" Aegeus began but was silenced immediately as Hadrian put up a hand.

"How *dare* you speak to my guest in that way." Hadrian was fuming, he'd stepped partly in front of Antinous as if to physically shield his lover from the hateful words Aegeus was spewing. Aegeus' eyes widened as he realized what Hadrian had heard.

"Yes, I heard everything you just said and you had better think twice before saying whatever was just about to spew from your hateful maw."

Hadrian could see the conflict on Aegeus' face clear as day. He didn't want to go against Hadrian, especially in public, but he clearly didn't agree that he should be reprimanded right now.

For the sake of not disturbing the celebration as well as preserving whatever pride Aegeus still had, Hadrian didn't raise his voice above a whisper, but the effect was the same.

"I don't care what your opinions are," Hadrian continued. "And you should count yourself lucky that I chose not to interfere earlier with your quota on oil production because I guarantee that it would not have gone your way."

Aegeus' eyes widened even further, snapping his mouth shut.

"Yes, those people I just spoke to informed me that you're currently going through a drought and the quota has left many families without enough water. I told you that I wouldn't interfere with the decision already made, however you and I will be having a long talk when we get back about ways that you can further support your community.

Additionally, it has become abundantly clear to me that you do not care one bit about people whom you consider to be lower status than you both by your blatant disregard for the safety and wellbeing of your people and how I just heard you speaking to Antinous.

Let me make myself perfectly plain, if I ever hear you speaking that way to him again, you will have far more to worry about than citizens protesting a quota you've installed."

Hadrian finished his rant and stood, staring down at the Athenian man. Aegeus had a look about him as though he had been physically struck by Hadrian's words.

"Do I make myself clear?" Hadrian growled out.

"Yes," Aegeus replied meekly. "Yes, of course."

"You are dismissed," Hadrian hissed out from between gritted teeth. With that, Aegeus turned tail and started off in the other direction with some of his guards. He had rightly assumed that he was not welcome in Hadrian's presence for the time being and it would be best to remove himself.

Hadrian was so angry that he almost didn't register the hand on his arm. But he did.

Turning his head, he saw Antinous watching him with concern.

"Sire," Felix said into his ear. "Perhaps we should move this conversation to a nearby courtyard or garden."

"Yes." Hadrian nodded. "You're right."

With Antinous still hanging onto his arm, Hadrian followed Felix into a nearby garden, hidden by a wall of vines. Felix stopped at the gate and instructed the other guards to post up nearby before standing in the archway and turning his back on the couple.

Hadrian pulled Antinous close, burying his face in the other man's curly locks.

"I'm sorry," he murmured, "I shouldn't have left you alone with him."

"It's fine," Antinous grumbled, loosely hanging his arms around Hadrian's waist.

"It's not," Hadrian contested. "When we first started this, we figured that I would be put in the line of fire for choosing to spend my time with you in this way. But I never considered the possibility that you would become a target like this and that was my fault, I should have anticipated it."

"Hadrian- I..." Antinous sighed. "I did anticipate it."

Pulling back so that he could see Antinous' face, Hadrian placed his hands on Antinous' shoulders. "You did?"

"Yes." Antinous shrugged. "I didn't want you to worry so I didn't say anything, but I always knew it would be a possibility."

"You knew and you still wanted to go through with it?" Hadrian couldn't help but cup Antinous' cheek with one hand.

"Of course. There are always going to be people who are unhappy with our choices, but that doesn't mean we shouldn't make them."

Hadrian felt the muscles in his jaw clench. He didn't deserve this man.

"I love you."

Antinous lifted his gaze to meet Hadrian's eyes as he listened.

"I don't think I've ever really loved anyone before and it may be soon, but I just keep thinking to myself that..."

"I love you, too."

"Really?" Hadrian tightened his grip on Antinous' shoulders.

"Yes of course." Antinous laughed, reaching up and taking Hadrian's face in his hands. "And that's why, it doesn't matter what Aegeus or anyone else says. I love you and there isn't a single thing that could possibly happen to make being with you not worth it."

Hadrian swallowed, fighting back tears as he pulled Antinous in for another embrace. "I feel the same way."

"Well good." The shorter man laughed. "I'm glad we are on the same page then. Shall we head back to the festival?"

Hadrian smiled and pressed a kiss to the top of Antinous' head. "Yes, let's."

CHAPTER TEN

They didn't see Aegeus for a while after that and by the time he circled back, he seemed to have gotten his priorities in order, reverting back to the cool politician he had been prior to his spat with Antinous. Of course, Hadrian was still going to keep an eye on him, but it seemed like the worst had passed.

After the parade ended, the group migrated to another area of town where other performers were providing entertainment during the frivolity.

When it was time for the feast, Hadrian had almost completely forgotten about the fight from earlier and Aegeus seemed more relaxed as well. During the feast, the priests came by and brought those looking to participate in the mysteries one at a time back to the temple for their participation in the Lesser Mysteries.

When it was Hadrian's turn, he kissed Antinous on the cheek and followed the priest out of the hall and into the back of the temple. He wasn't sure exactly what he was to expect, but he'd gotten through a majority of his life just rolling with the punches and taking things as they came so he figured that this was no different.

The priests led him back into a chamber off the side of the main temple and closed the door behind him. In the room were three other individuals; one Dadouchos and two Dadouchousa Priestesses.

The Dadouchos stood in the center of the room with a torch. On one side of him, the Priestess held a piglet, and on the other side, the Priestess held a knife.

"By participating in these rites, you swear to uphold a vow of secrecy. Once you leave this room, the gods will determine if you are worthy to move on."

Hadrian nodded. He was familiar with the practices of these pagan temples as it was the primary religion of the common people and what he had practiced as a child.

The priest looked to the priestesses and nodded, allowing them to walk forward and place the piglet and knife in front of him.

"You will now sacrifice the piglet to Demeter and Persephone, then bathe in the river Ilissos to cleanse yourself. Do you accept?"

Hadrian considered the piglet for a moment before picking up the knife. In one swift movement, he slit the piglet's throat and said a little prayer under his breath to Demeter and Persephone.

As he raised his head, the priest nodded and gestured for him to progress to the door on the other side of the room. As he opened the door, he saw that it seemed to be a spring of some sort.

"Here part of the river Ilissos flows. Cleanse yourself and then you may leave."

The priest stepped aside so he could enter and then closed the door, leaving him alone.

Hadrian dropped his robes and stepped naked into the river, allowing the feeling of the current to sweep over his torso and legs for a moment before dunking his head. Holding himself underwater for a moment, Hadrian allowed the current to sweep over him, cleansing him of his sins. Then, he stood, allowing the water to roll off his back in droplets.

He stepped out of the river and used the cloth hanging on the wall to dry himself off as best he could before putting his clothes back on. His beard was still damp but it wasn't drenched, it would likely dry with the evening breeze.

Turning back to the wall, he noticed a second door that he hadn't seen originally upon entering the space. He assumed that was the door they were talking about when they told him to exit the space.

As he left through the secondary door, he found himself in a hallway that led back to the feast. The hallway was lined with torches held by various artistic visages of either Demeter or Persephone and for a moment, Hadrian actually took the time to appreciate this place for what it was.

He'd been so distracted throughout the day with the festivities, everything that was going on with Aegeus, and the feast that he'd been distracted from the true purpose of this ceremony. It truly was a celebration of love and two people returning to each other no matter what.

Regardless of Persephone's new home in the underworld with Hades, she always came back in the spring to be with her mother Demeter, who welcomed her with open arms. It made him think of his parents and how his mother had always prayed to their altar each night. It made him think of home and his people, but now, it also made him think of Antinous.

It was the thought of Antinous that got him moving again and headed back to the main hall. However, when he got there, Antinous was nowhere to be seen.

He sat back down in his spot and leaned over to Felix. Almost as if Felix knew exactly what he was going to ask, he replied proactively.

"They took him to participate about a minute ago."

"Ah." Hadrian nodded, turning back to his plate.

"So, how was it?" Felix asked, taking a drink of his wine.

"Oh, you know." Hadrian grinned bashfully. "Damp."

Felix cracked a smile that he attempted to hide with his wine glass.

"So, you really don't have to go through the first mystery again?" Hadrian continued, getting back to his food.

"No, you really only have to be chosen to move forward once and then you can return again and again as many times as you like to participate in the higher mysteries." Felix shrugged. "My parents were devoted followers of Demeter and in an attempt to keep me in touch as long as they could, they put me through the rites when I was young, to learn the valuable lesson of children always returning to their parents."

Hadrian chuckled. "How did that go?"

Felix shrugged, an amused look on his face. "About as well as you might expect. I drop by whenever I'm in the vicinity and while it's not as often as my mother would like I'm sure, she knows I do the best I can."

Hadrian hummed in acknowledgment. "Wouldn't want to incur the wrath of the gods now would we?"

Felix's lip twitched up a little in response. "More like, wouldn't want to incur the wrath of my mother."

Hadrian smiled and settled back into his seat, falling into a comfortable silence with Felix. Felix had been at his side for nearly 20 years now and they knew how to exist in each other's presence.

A few minutes later, Hadrian turned as Antinous touched his shoulder.

He looked the same save for the droplets of water in his hair glistening in the candle light.

"Hello," Hadrian greeted Antinous as he sat down. "Cleansed is a good look on you."

Antinous rolled his eyes and met Hadrian's gaze before reaching up and touching his beard. "I could say the same about you."

Hadrian smiled, pouring Antinous another glass of wine. "Anything too unexpected?"

"No." Antinous shook his head, taking a drink from his goblet. "It's about what I would expect from an initiation rite for a temple dedicated to the goddess of the harvest."

At that moment, someone across the table pulled Antinous' attention away, involving him in conversation about how he was enjoying the festival. Hadrian felt Felix lean in slightly so Hadrian alone could hear him.

"You know, he's really good for you."

Hadrian didn't bother to turn his attention away from watching his lover. "Yeah, I know."

"I don't think I've ever seen you this happy," Felix continued, "I know it goes without saying but, I just wanted you to know that I'll protect him."

Hadrian swallowed, a lump forming in his throat. "I know." He paused. "Thank you, Felix."

Felix grunted in response and turned back to his plate. This whole day had been overwhelming to a degree, first the argument between him and Aegeus, then telling Antinous he loved him, and now this whole sacrificing a suckling pig thing. As happy as he was that Antinous was having a great time, he felt an overwhelming sense of relief at the fact that the Greater Mysteries were not happening until tomorrow night.

He was just settling in to ride out the rest of the evening when Antinous turned back towards him and laid a hand on his thigh.

"Come on," Antinous prompted.

"Where?" Hadrian raised an eyebrow. "Aren't you having fun?"

"Of course I am." Antinous grinned back. "But someone promised me that we would get some flowers on the way back tonight and I wanted to catch the vendors before they closed up for the night."

Hadrian smiled, placing a hand over Antinous'. He had a sneaking suspicion that Antinous knew he was burnt out on being social and was doing this for his benefit, but he was more than happy to play along. Especially if it gave them some alone time.

"Ah, yes. I did say that." Turning to Felix, he lowered his voice. "We are heading back."

Felix nodded and wiped his mouth, walking with them as they made their way out of the hall. After they left, however, Felix made himself scarce.

"Where did Felix go?" Antinous asked, looking around.

"He's giving us some space," Hadrian replied, hooking Antinous' arm through his own. "Trying not to eavesdrop and watching from the shadows."

"That's both sweet and creepy," Antinous joked, tightening his grip on Hadrian's arm.

"You know," Hadrian continued as they made their way down the street. "Felix approves of our relationship."

They meandered down the cobblestones, back toward the vendors. Lanterns had made their way out and shone in different colors covering the ground. Hadrian had been to hundreds of festivals in his time as emperor, but never had he truly felt the beauty of the atmosphere as much as he did now, with Antinous.

This was not a new feeling, but rather something that had been building for quite some time. He realized recently that whenever Antinous was around him he felt lighter, food tasted better, sensations were more intense, and everything seemed so much more brightly colored. It was almost as if, by having Antinous at his side, he was able to experience life to the fullest degree in a way he never had before.

"He does?" Antinous piped up.

"Mhm." Hadrian made a noise of affirmation, peeking down at his younger lover. Antinous seemed genuinely relieved as he let out a breath.

"I'm glad." Antinous rested his head on Hadrian's arm as they walked. "I just assumed that most people, if not everyone, would find our relationship strange. Then, after the whole thing with Aegeus, I felt a little less confident."

"I never want you to doubt what we have."

"It's not that." Antinous shook his head softly. "It's just, I don't want to cause you problems. But with all my concern, I forgot for a moment that you are a powerful man yourself." He laughed.

Hadrian scrunched his nose in fake offense.

"But today when you called out Aegeus and he ran like a scared child, it just reminded me that you don't need me to protect you."

Hadrian felt a weight lift off his heart. He had been worried that the interaction earlier today with Aegeus had shaken Antinous, but seemingly it has only worked to further solidify their bond.

"I will always have your back," Antinous continued, "And I know that you'll have mine, but it made me feel more confident knowing that our relationship isn't costing you the respect of your subjects."

Hadrian felt awful that Antinous had been seeing himself as a potential detriment to his rule, but he did understand where the other man was coming from. So, he decided to let it go for now as they finally found themselves in front of several flower stalls.

"Do you have any specific colors in mind?" Hadrian prompted, tilting his head towards the vendors.

"Mmm." Antinous hummed thoughtfully. "My mom always got red flowers, because they were representative of Persephone's pomegranate."

"But?" Hadrian asked, sensing that there was more the shorter man wanted to say.

Antinous turned his head and smiled. "But, I always thought it might be nice to get something darker too."

"Why's that?"

"Because I know she's coming back to be with her mother, but I always wondered if she missed Hades while she was away. So, if we had something darker, it might remind her of home and help the transition feel easier."

Hadrian's heart melted. "You are truly one of a kind, you know that?"

Antinous chuckled. "I have been told that, yes."

Hadrian reached down and tilted Antinous' chin up, leaning down and pressing a soft kiss to his lips, before standing back up and addressing the vendor in front of them.

"We will take some of those roses and some of those violets. If you could make us a bouquet with half of each and add some greenery in there, we will take that."

"We should also add some of that wheat, for Demeter." Antinous piped up, pointing to an area towards the back.

"You heard him." Hadrian laughed, nodding at the vendor.

Once they had paid for their flowers, Antinous held onto them like they were the most precious thing in the world and extended his other hand to hold Hadrian's. Then, together they made their way back to the palace.

CHAPTER ELEVEN

As they entered the palace grounds, Felix caught up and followed them to their quarters.

"I'll post some guards outside." Felix spoke softly to Hadrian as they retired for the night.

Hadrian nodded and smiled. "Thank you."

Felix hummed and turned to walk away. Felix always understood what Hadrian was trying to say without needing clarification, so Hadrian knew that Felix understood that he had meant thank you for more than just posting the guards.

"Hang on," Hadrian called into the room, shutting and locking the door, "let's find a place to put those."

There was a dresser near one of the windows that already had a vase sitting empty on the surface. So, Antinous walked over and put the flowers into the vase, stepping back to inspect his work.

Hadrian came up behind him and wrapped his arms around the younger man, kissing his neck. "They look beautiful."

Antinous hummed happily, leaning into the touch. "So I know that you don't want to go to sleep yet, what do you want to do in the meantime?"

Hadrian tightened his hold on Antinous and nipped gently at his neck. "I have a couple of ideas."

"Oh do you?" Antinous teased, turning around in Hadrian's embrace and throwing his arms up around his shoulders.

"Maybe." Hadrian smiled, leaning down to press his lips against Antinous'. He kissed him deeply, letting one of his hands sink lower on his back toward his full ass.

Antinous hummed against his lips and pressed into him. "I think I like this plan."

"I thought you might," Hadrian joked, migrating his kisses across Antinous' face towards his jaw and then down his neck. He felt Antinous melt against him as his pulse sped up. Reaching down with his other hand, Hadrian picked Antinous up and wrapped his thighs around his waist, migrating them over to the bed.

As they moved, Hadrian kissed and nipped at Antinous' neck, feeling his hardness growing against his abs. With the smaller man's legs around him, he couldn't hide anything as he grew, winding his hands up in Hadrian's hair.

When they finally got to the bed, Hadrian used one hand to guide them down, laying Antinous on his back and climbing on top of him. He moved his mouth up to Antinous' lips again, kissing him deeply before retreating back down between his legs.

"I never did get to return the favor," Hadrian murmured as he ran a hand over the bulging fabric at Antinous' crotch.

Antinous' breath hitched and his hips twitched upwards at the touch. "Fuck, Hadrian... are you going to suck me off?"

"I warn you," Hadrian replied, grinning and looking up at his lover, "this will be a first for me so I may need you to coach me through it."

Antinous groaned, his cock twitching. "I know you mean it, but I don't think you understand how fucking hot that is."

Hadrian leaned forward, nuzzling Antinous' cock through his clothes before pulling them off and biting his lip as he watched Antinous' now leaking cock hover above his stomach. He knew that he could probably figure out the basics but now that Antinous had expressed interest in telling him what to do, he decided to take full advantage of that.

"Whenever you're ready." He teased, grinning up at Antinous.

Antinous groaned, rubbing his hands over his face and murmuring something that sounded suspiciously like, 'you're gonna kill me'.

"Alright." Antinous stuck a pillow under his back and sat up on his elbows. "Um."

Hadrian just made himself comfortable between the other man's thighs and enjoyed the view of Antinous trying to decide where he wanted him to start.

"Use your hand to jerk me off a couple of times first."

Hadrian obeyed immediately, wrapping his fingers around Antinous' erection and reveling in the shudder that went through Antinous' body as he stroked him.

"Then, uh…" Antinous stuttered. His eyes hooded over as he watched. "Lick the tip a couple of times."

Hadrian leaned forward and intentionally stuck out his tongue teasingly close to Antinous' cock, pausing for a moment before giving the head a couple of kitten licks. The second he did, he felt Antinous' abs tense and his cock twitch in his hand.

"Oh, fuck… yeah, that's good," Antinous groaned, running one hand through his hair. "Then, just keep your hand still for a minute and suck on the head."

Hadrian obliged, stilling his movements with his hand and leaned down further, taking the head of Antinous' cock into his mouth and sucking lightly. Then, unprompted, he used his tongue to circle around it while he sucked.

Antinous' breath was speeding up and as Hadrian looked up, he was met with Antinous' hungry gaze as he watched.

"Yes, fuck… Hadrian…" Antinous moaned. "Now, use your hand on the shaft and slowly start taking more into your mouth."

Hadrian started moving his hand again, bobbing his head with the movements as he took more and more of Antinous' length into his mouth with each iteration.

"Fuck, you're so hot." Antinous panted, watching Hadrian suck him off.

Admittedly, this whole situation was getting Hadrian a little hot and bothered himself. He had never considered the possibility that he would enjoy giving head before since the only other people he had been with were consorts who were dedicated exclusively to his pleasure, but it definitely seemed like it was a turn on for him.

With his other hand, Hadrian reached between his own legs and palmed himself through his clothes.

"Oh shit." Antinous' eyes followed Hadrian's hand and he bit his lip as Hadrian's hand reached its destination. "Are you touching yourself right now?"

Hadrian hummed affirmatively, closing his eyes for a minute, taking in the melody of moans that escaped Antinous' lips.

"Fuck," Antinous cursed, rocking his hips slightly in time with Hadrian's ministrations.

Hadrian wasn't quite sure what his gag reflex looked like, but he wasn't willing to test it tonight. Luckily, his hand prevented Antinous from thrusting too deeply into his mouth.

"Oh gods," Antinous groaned. "Just um, keep doing that, yeah and maybe tug on my balls a little."

Bringing his other hand back up towards Antinous, Hadrian took hold of Antinous' balls and gave them a gentle tug.

"Ah... harder..." Antinous begged, the rocking of his hips becoming more pronounced.

Getting a better grip, Hadrian pulled more firmly, pleased with the noise it elicited from his lover. It was a mixture between a sound of pain and pleasure, but Hadrian trusted that Antinous wouldn't have asked for anything he didn't want and he wanted this to be as good for him as possible.

So he continued sucking while maintaining the consistent pressure with his other hand.

"Ah- Hadrian... yes... it's so good."

Hadrian couldn't help the moan that escaped his lips as he rubbed his own hard cock up against the bedding. His jaw was beginning to ache, but it wasn't anything he wasn't willing to go through to witness this incredible scene of Antinous spread on his back, begging for him.

"I'm so close." Antinous panted. The movement of his hips began to stutter slightly, but Hadrian maintained his own speed, sucking a little harder with each movement.

Antinous voice rang out, getting louder and louder in volume as he approached the edge. Then, suddenly his hips stopped and the younger man gasped.

"Fuck, fuck, fuck, fuck... quick, let go of my balls and suck me down as far as you can."

Without hesitation, Hadrian released his grip on Antinous' balls and sucked as much of his cock down as he could. He could feel Antinous cock throb as he came, and he tasted the salty cum hitting the back of his throat. However, instead of pulling off, he just swallowed and continued sucking through each wave, until Antinous was writhing on the bed.

"Fuck, baby… okay, okay, okay stop now." Antinous begged and Hadrian obeyed, grinning as he wiped his mouth with the back of his hand.

He crawled up the bed and lay next to Antinous on his side, pulling him in. Antinous nuzzled into Hadrian's neck and sighed.

"That was amazing."

Hadrian chuckled and squeezed him tighter. "Good, amazing was what I was going for."

Antinous laughed into Hadrian's shoulder, hugging Hadrian tightly before slipping his hand down between them and cupping Hadrian's cock. The touch immediately cut off Hadrian's laughter, changing it into a gasp. He'd forgotten for a moment how hopelessly turned on he was.

"Gods, I want this cock," Antinous mumbled, giving it another squeeze.

"You sure you're alright for another round?" Hadrian asked, measuring his breathing.

"Oh, yes." Antinous pulled back and met Hadrian's gaze. "I want you inside me so bad."

"Shit," Hadrian cursed, following Antinous' lead until they were both further up on the bed. He reached for his lover only for Antinous to sneak just out of reach and shake his head.

"No, no." Antinous grinned mischievously, pulling off the rest of his clothes. "I'm going to prepare myself for you and you are going to watch."

Hadrian groaned, feeling his cock throb.

Antinous was so beautiful, he looked like he could be chiseled from marble as he turned to the side and reached behind himself. As Antinous slid a finger inside himself, Hadrian pulled off his own clothes and settled back against the pillows, cock in hand.

Antinous made sure that Hadrian was always in his field of vision as he fucked himself with his fingers, slowly adding more and more until he was riding three fingers, face flushed, and fully hard again.

Hadrian couldn't help but stroke his cock just to relieve some of the pressure from the absolutely sinful scene in front of him.

"Do you like watching me fuck myself?" Antinous moaned, arching his back.

"Absolutely," Hadrian replied with no hesitation. He spread his legs and moved his hand away from his cock. "Can't you tell how much?"

Antinous whined and sat up, letting his fingers slip out of him. "I can't take it anymore, I need you."

Hadrian shifted, moving to his knees and meeting Antinous halfway, their lips crashing together. Their breaths mingled as they panted, touching each other everywhere they could, barely separating to breathe.

"How do you want it baby?" Hadrian asked, grabbing at Antinous' ass, dragging his finger around the ring of muscle.

"Ah..." Antinous arched his back, pressing himself down onto Hadrian's finger slightly. "Behind... I want you to take me from the back."

"Mmmm." Hadrian nodded. In one swift movement, Hadrian took Antinous by the waist and flipped him so he was face down on the bed.

"Oh shit." Antinous mumbled into the sheets as he arched his back further presenting his ass to Hadrian.

Hadrian grabbed his cock and rubbed it against Antinous' ass, just barely catching his hole each time before pulling back.

"Please, please, please..." Antinous begged, trying everything in his power to get Hadrian inside of him.

Hadrian bit his lip and tilted his cock, pressing the head against Antinous' hole, teasing him for a moment before pressing all the way in. The movement took the wind out of both of them for a moment. Hadrian just waited, his hips flush with Antinous' ass. He wanted to fuck into him more than anything, but he wanted to make sure that he didn't hurt the other man.

"You alright?" He checked, noting how strained his voice sounded in the moment.

"Yes, yes, I'm fine," Antinous said as quickly as he could. "Please fuck me."

"Oh, thank the gods," Hadrian murmured before pulling almost completely out and slamming back in. Sucking Antinous off and then watching him prep himself had stretched out his self control to the thinnest it could possibly get and he was so hard he could cut diamonds.

Hands on Antinous' hips, Hadrian fucked into Antinous over and over again, never slowing and never letting up for a moment. He was only spurred on further as he saw Antinous reach between his legs and start stroking himself wildly in time with the thrusts.

"I'm so close." Hadrian got out between gritted teeth. He could feel his balls tightening up and his blood start to go cold the way it did the split second before orgasm.

"Yes, yes!" Antinous moaned. "Cum inside me, fuck."

In that moment, Hadrian couldn't have staved off his orgasm if he tried. He tipped over the edge, slamming into Antinous one final time before pumping him full. As he came, he rocked his hips gently to maintain the friction, but cried out in pleasure one more time as Antinous tipped over the edge as well, clenching around him.

He wasn't even sure how it was possible, but as Antinous came, Hadrian felt another shock wave rush through him, cumming even more.

Immediately after it was over, Hadrian felt all the strength leave his body. He leaned over Antinous and wrapped an arm around the other man's torso, pressing kisses to Antinous' back.

Antinous moved forward, letting Hadrian slip out of him before returning to his embrace and together they lay down, wrapped in each other's arms.

"I think that was the best sex I've ever had," Antinous admitted after a couple of minutes of silence.

Hadrian laughed. "Me too."

"I have never had someone let me coach them through a blowjob but, gods are you a fast learner. Are you sure that was your first time doing that?"

Hadrian chuckled and hummed affirmatively. "Never wanted to before."

"Well, let's hope you'll want to again because I don't think I could live with myself if the world never experienced your masterful skills ever again."

"If you want me to blow you more often, all you have to do is ask," Hadrian replied teasingly.

"Well, shit. If that's all it takes," Antinous replied.

The next moment they both burst out laughing, just holding on to each other. When they finally calmed down, Hadrian ran a hand over Antinous' cheek and kissed him softly on the lips.

"Come on. Let's get cleaned up. I'd hate to get the sheets dirty before we sleep here."

"I think that ship has already sailed," Antinous replied.

Chapter Twelve

Hadrian woke up much earlier than he had planned. Whether it was the sun streaming in the window or the brisk morning air, he felt moved to go for a walk. Hopping up, he threw on some clothes and made his way out to the terrace attached to his room.

The terrace was connected to the inner gardens of the palace so Hadrian took the steps down from his room to the rose garden below.

He'd always loved spring. Not only because the weather was typically more tolerable than it was in winter and summer, but also because of the way everything bloomed. He'd never truly felt comfortable at the palace in Rome, first because everything around him just reminded him that his parents were dead, but then because the palace became synonymous with where his wife was.

They bickered. And not in a fun, playful way. Hadrian had tried to be a good husband to her but it just seemed like everything he ever did, every choice he ever made was wrong. He tried buying her gifts; they were never exactly what she wanted. He tried spending quality time with her; she was always quiet and grumpy during their excursions and never contributed to the conversation. He tried complimenting her; she would roll her eyes.

Eventually, he realized that she was in a much better mood when he'd been away for a while, so he just started leaving her alone.

When he got the idea to start traveling to see more of his empire, he didn't even ask her what she thought about it. He knew that she would enjoy having the palace to herself, besides, it's not like she'd wanted to be married to him in the first place.

In all the years he had been traveling, he had never once missed the palace; never once missed the cold stares of his wife that he would catch when he turned a corner. He never felt the need to settle down because there wasn't ever anything to go back to.

However, as he stood in the garden and looked at the roses, he thought to himself that it might be nice to have somewhere with a garden to return to. He and Antinous could plant flowers to set out for their altars and have fruit trees that they could tend to and pick every year.

It probably wouldn't be in Rome, but maybe somewhere on the coast, near Naples.

His daydreaming was interrupted by the sound of footsteps making their way down one of the paths. When he turned, a messenger had stopped just short of him, bowing deeply.

"Letters for you, Sire."

"Thank you." Hadrian took the letters and looked down at the envelopes as the messenger scurried away.

One read in simple gold writing, "Hadrian", the other "Antinous".

He could guess what they could possibly be about but since Antinous had received one too, he figured they should probably open them together. As he was making his way back to the terrace, a sleepy Antinous wrapped in a sheet appeared on the balcony.

"Good morning, love," Hadrian called, making his way up the steps.

"Mmm morning," Antinous replied sleepily, meeting Hadrian at the top of the steps and melting into his embrace. "I woke up and you were gone."

"I'm sorry." Hadrian hugged him more firmly and pressed a kiss to his forehead. "I was going for a walk through the garden, but I was actually just on my way back to wake you. We got letters."

This perked Antinous up a little, lifting his gaze and tilting his head to the side. "We did?"

"Yes." Hadrian handed Antinous his letter and walked them inside, one arm still around the smaller man's shoulders.

"I assume they're from the priesthood regarding the Greater Mysteries later today."

Antinous jumped onto the bed and crossed his legs, opening the letter with excitement.

"Oh! Hadrian, they want us to continue our participation!"

Antinous was practically vibrating with excitement. "I wonder what kind of super secret ritual we will get to be privy to tonight."

"Who knows?" Hadrian replied, opening his own letter. "Maybe we will get to slaughter an adult pig this time."

Antinous laughed and Hadrian pulled the letter out of the envelope. It was simple, adorned with the same gold handwriting.

Tonight.
Greater Mysteries.

Hadrian flipped the card over, looking for some sort of location but found nothing.

"Strange." Hadrian hummed. "It doesn't seem like they are going to tell us where to meet them."

"Of course not." Antinous grinned mischievously. "It wouldn't be very mysterious if they did, would it?"

Hadrian laughed, tossing his letter onto the bed before caging Antinous between his arms. "I suppose not."

Antinous grinned back and wrapped his arms around Hadrian's neck, pulling him into a kiss.

"Mmm." Hadrian hummed into the kiss, pulling back before it got too intense. "Come on, I'm sure there's breakfast waiting."

Antinous sighed and got up off the bed. "Perfect, I was just thinking about how I might just die if I don't get food in the next ten minutes."

The pair finished getting dressed and made their way down to the great hall. To Hadrian's surprise, Aegeus was nowhere to be found, but it seemed as though breakfast was being served anyway.

It was probably for the best this way, Aegeus had been getting on Hadrian's last nerve and the less he had to see of him the better. The peace only lasted so long, however. After about 20 minutes, Aegeus came storming in, a frown affixed on his face.

Antinous and Hadrian exchanged glances, shrugging subtly.

He didn't seem to want to talk about it and immediately dug into his plate, ignoring the conversation happening around the table.

"He didn't get invited back for the Greater Mysteries." Helena, the woman to Hadrian's right leaned over and whispered to him. "Orpheus got his letter this morning and when he found out they'd already been delivered and he didn't receive one, he went directly to the temple to demand they had made a mistake. From the looks of it, it didn't go very well."

Hadrian hummed in acknowledgment and picked up more food with his fork. He wasn't sure what the criteria had been that the priests were looking for, but he was secretly a little happy that Aegeus did not qualify. Not that he would ever say it out loud, however.

"I'm sure you got invited back though, right sir?" Helena continued.

"I did," Hadrian replied. "Antinous and I both got our letters this morning."

"What?" Aegeus' voice rang throughout the hall and suddenly all other conversation came to a halt.

Hadrian looked up to see Aegeus red faced and seething, a fork and knife grasped in his white knuckled hands.

"Are you seriously telling me that HE got an invitation and I did not?"

Hadrian wiped his mouth with his napkin and put down his utensils. "Well, technically I was not telling you anything. You happened to eavesdrop on the conversation."

Aegeus slammed his fists down on the table and stood up. "Those crackpot priests have no idea what they are doing, the fact that I was not invited back but this lowly servant whore-"

"That. Is ENOUGH!" Hadrian stood with such presence and force that Aegeus flinched back a little. "I have been lenient with you, Aegeus, I thought that a softer touch would allow for better communication and partnership between us but it seems I was mistaken. I warned you that if you spoke that way about Antinous again I would not stand for it."

Hadrian pushed back his chair and walked across the room over to Aegeus. "Perhaps leadership is too much of a burden for you Aegeus, since you seem far more concerned about your admittance to a particular group than you do about the well being of your citizens.

"We will be leaving first thing tomorrow morning as I do not wish to spend any more time in this pool of hate you have created. That being said, I will be leaving a detachment behind to make sure you behave yourself until the counsel I will be summoning from the capitol arrives to relieve you of your duties."

Aegeus' eyes widened as he realized his mistake and he opened his mouth to reply, but Hadrian wasn't done.

"Of course, you will still be able to live in your palace and act as a figurehead, as long as you BEHAVE. I have never been one to interfere with the ruling of individual areas of my territory but I feel that I would be a neglectful leader if I allow you to continue.

However, if I hear that you give even one infinitesimal amount of hardship to the detachment or counsel, I will have you removed from this palace so fast you won't even have time to protest. I gave you an opportunity to fix your attitude yesterday, but you will not be receiving another."

The silence in the chamber was palpable as Hadrian finished scolding Aegeus in front of his entire court.

"Sir. I-" Aegeus tried.

"No. It is far too late for apologies or amends." Hadrian turned and walked back to his side of the table. "You have shown the quality of your character to me in the past few days I have been here with you and I have to say, I don't like it and apparently, neither do the priests. Have you perhaps stopped to consider the possibility that you did not get invited back because you are NOT in fact worthy?"

Aegeus swallowed, shutting his mouth.

"That is what I thought." Hadrian shook his head. "People like you always put the blame on others without ever looking in a mirror and wondering if perhaps they are the ones doing something wrong."

Hadrian shook his head and sighed.

"I think that we will be spending the rest of the day out on the town. Felix? Please send word to Rome that Gaius is to make his way here post haste. I will leave the detachment details up to you."

Felix nodded and spoke softly to the soldier next to him who, in turn, scurried off.

Hadrian looked down at Antinous who had also risen at this point and took his hand.

"Come on." Antinous nodded and followed as Hadrian led them out of the palace and into the gardens out front.

He knew that Felix and some of his other soldiers were following them but he didn't so much as pause to make sure they were keeping up. They walked in silence for about ten minutes until they reached the water.

Hadrian was still burning, absolutely infuriated with the interaction that had just occurred, but he focused on his breathing, trying his best to calm down.

As though sensing that he was still struggling, Antinous didn't say anything, but rather just put his arms around Hadrian's waist and rested his head on his chest. Hadrian wrapped his arms around the smaller man and let his presence calm his heartbeat.

The waves on the shore helped him measure his breath and as he looked out on the water, he felt himself coming down from the anger and reaching equilibrium again.

"I'm going to be honest." Hadrian broke the silence. "I cannot remember the last time I was that angry."

"Well," Antinous replied, not moving from his spot in Hadrian's arms. "I feel very cared about that you got that angry on my behalf."

Hadrian smiled softly.

"I know as your partner, I should be encouraging you to practice patience and forgiveness, leading you to be a better person and all, but I can't say that I'm upset you put him in his place. He really was a colossal asshole."

Laughter bubbled up from Hadrian's chest and pretty soon, he was just trying to catch his breath from the sheer force of laughter. Then, Antinous was laughing too, together they laughed hysterically until they were clutching their sides, doubled over.

The moment he could get control of himself, Hadrian wiped the corner of his eye and took a deep breath.

"I don't know what I would do without you," Hadrian confessed. "Really."

Antinous cocked his head and gave him a soft smile.

"After my parents died, I was just so focused on being the good son Trajan needed me to be that I think I lost a bit of myself in the process. It's a lot of pressure, training to be emperor, especially for someone as young as I was and

I think that I felt as though I owed Trajan for taking me in. So I couldn't really afford to be overwhelmed.

I needed to always do exactly what was asked of me and that included everything I was taught about diplomatic relations and how to handle contentious situations like that. It didn't seem like a lot at first, just an improved table habit here and an extra bow there, but it was slowly chipping away at me.

By the time he suggested I marry Vibia, I don't think it even occurred to me to have an opinion on it, let alone be against it. She so very clearly hated me, any normal person would have turned her away as an option for both of our sakes, but the only thing I was thinking about was doing as Trajan asked and being the good son that I knew he wanted."

Hadrian paused, looking out at the water.

"Everyone always told me how lucky I was. Being plucked out of poverty like that by the emperor, and I just took them at face value. I didn't think about the things it would cost me in the long term. When someone shows up at your door and offers you everything, you don't think about the things you might lose because you don't have anything to give.

By the time Trajan died, I just was so entrenched that I never questioned it. I just kept thinking, what would Trajan do? Would he be proud of the choices I'm making?

I never stopped to think about what I wanted or how I thought I should do things. When I first started losing sleep over it all, I was told that it was just the pressure of running an empire and not to worry about it. But I think, I think that it was my soul's way of telling me that I had been on autopilot for too long and that I needed to wake up."

Hadrian turned to Antinous.

"And then I met you and... you saved me from myself. Showing me that I was worthy of being loved and loving in return and I have to tell you, Antinous." Hadrian took Antinous' face in his hands and pressed their foreheads together. "Since you came into my life, I've never slept so well."

CHAPTER THIRTEEN

As the sun began to set, merchants began bringing in their set ups and everyone seemed to be making their way home. Hadrian and Antinous walked hand in hand down the bank of the river, meandering with no particular direction in mind.

After they had left the palace, Hadrian had informed Felix to have someone let them know should the priesthood try to contact them with details about the mysteries while they were not there. However, no one had come to inform them of anything yet. The card had been quite cryptic, only stating "tonight" as a time and completely leaving out the detail of "where."

The priests had to have some way of getting the additional information to the participants already planned out. So Hadrian just opted not to worry.

By the time the sun had fully set, they had made their way down to the older part of town just off the river when they caught sight of lanterns standing outside of a smaller temple by the water. As they approached, a priest stepped out of the shadows and smiled, gesturing towards the entrance.

"Emperor Hadrian, Antinous, Felix. Welcome, we knew you would find your way."

Hadrian blinked a couple of times in confusion, exchanging glances with Antinous before the smaller man spoke up.

"This is the location of the Greater Mysteries, isn't it?"

The priest didn't say anything in response, but rather instead smiled quietly and gestured towards the entrance to the temple again.

Together, with Felix following silently behind them, they passed by the priest and walked across the threshold of the temple.

"Strange." Antinous commented. "I wasn't really thinking about where we were going. What are the odds that we ended up right where we were supposed to be?"

Hadrian didn't respond, but rather just took Antinous' hand and continued their path down the hallway, into the temple. He had no idea what the odds were, especially considering that nobody who had been through the rites before had ever been allowed to talk about them once they'd been completed.

He didn't think that Felix had directed them anywhere, but somehow, he had also ended up here, right where he needed to be to participate in the Greater Mysteries once again. Glancing over to Felix, he didn't seem to know where he was going, but he also didn't seem surprised to have made it here.

"Perhaps it wasn't a coincidence at all," Hadrian mused.

As he finished his thought, the three of them made their way through an archway that led them to a circular space at the center of the temple. In the middle of the room was a large bowl with two pedestals, one on each side.

One of the pedestals held a chest while the other held a basket, both of equal size. The chest was made of what looked like Egyptian marble and had a complicated looking locking mechanism on the front. The basket was round and had no sort of locking mechanism to keep the lid on, but it remained closed all the same.

A few more stragglers made their way in, looking equally as confused as Hadrian felt before the priests closed the temple doors. In total there were ten of them, seven participants, two high priestesses, and one high priest.

The two priestesses made their way to the center of the room, each standing beside one of the pedestals. The high priest took a turn around the room, extinguishing the torches that were lighting up the space. By the time he was done, the only light in the room was coming from the moon shining in through the oculus at the top of the temple.

The priest poured ten glasses of a mysterious liquid in a pitcher that had been waiting on a shelf to the right side of the door. He then made his way around the circle, giving each participant a cup, one at a time.

When Hadrian got his, he dipped his face to smell the drink, expecting some sort of wine perhaps, but was surprised when he was met with an earthy smell. He couldn't quite put his finger on what it was, but it wasn't unpleasant. He glanced to the side and exchanged looks with Antinous; for whatever reason, doing this put him at ease.

Once each of the participants had their cup, the priest stopped in the center of the room and handed each of the priestesses their cups, leaving one for himself.

"As we drink tonight," he began, "we invite the wisdom of the mysteries to open us up to the possibility through the gods."

He nodded and each of the priestesses drank from their cups, finishing them in one go. He then nodded at the participants and following suit, Hadrian brought the cup up to his lips and drank it down.

It tasted of honey and barley, but also of something else that he could not quite place. In truth, he was thankful that it tasted as good as it did, all things considered, it could have been foul.

Once the group had finished their drinks, the priest poured the entirety of his cup into the bowl in the center of the room and tossed a torch in after, causing flame to erupt from the center of the temple.

Almost immediately, Hadrian could see the color of the flame changing, first from red to blue, then from blue to green, and again back to red. His body felt heavy, as though he had just ridden for three days straight, but at the same time, he felt strong in his stance. Unmoving and comfortable.

One of the priestesses threw her head back, mouth open in a gasp. She almost looked suspended in time for a moment before snapping back to attention. However, now, the way she stood was different. Where she had once been prostrate and humble, she now stood with a regal air about her. Without so much as even looking around the room, she reached forward to her basket and removed the lid, placing it to the side.

She reached inside the basket and pulled out a bronze snake, coiled, with its eyes dim. The way that the light of the fire danced off the scales almost made it seem like it was moving, rippling in her hands. She took one finger and stroked the snake from the top of the head, down its back to the tail.

Then, suddenly, and gradually, the snake raised its head, it's emerald green eyes lighting up. The priestess lifted the snake further, letting it uncoil and drape around her shoulders.

The second priestess was now sitting on her knees on the ground, head hanging heavily. The first priestess looked her over for a moment before making her way across the space, almost as if she was floating, and stopping directly in front of the second priestess. She knelt down beside her, taking her face in her hands and kissing her lightly on the lips.

This action seemed to breathe life into the second priestess and she sat up straight, lifting her gaze to the other woman. As she caught sight of the snake around her neck, her eyes softened in a manner of recognition.

She allowed the first woman to help her up off the floor and then stepped over to her box. She placed her fingers upon the box, and with just a touch, the click of the locking mechanism could be heard throughout the room.

Once the lock disengaged, the second priestess opened up the lid of the box and reached inside. Carefully, she pulled out a crown of flowers.

Not a crown of carved flowers, nor a crown of dead flowers, but a crown of live flowers that looked as though they had been picked that day.

Then, almost as if there was some sort of mirage shimmering over the body of the second priestess, the ghost of a floor length gown made itself known as well as a lovely, dark crown.

Giving no mind to the spectral nature of her garments, the second priestess reached up and plucked the crown off her head, placing it in the box. As she transitioned it from her head to the box, it seemed to gain more and more physicality until it was as real as the box itself. She picked up the flower crown and placed it on her head instead.

It took a couple of beats but then, pretty soon, it was ethereal just like the other had been. She then turned around to the first priestess and smiled, pulling her into an embrace. Together they walked to the center of the room and stood on either side of the bowl.

But then, for just a moment, the second priestess turned her head and her gaze landed directly on Antinous. She smiled warmly and nodded her head at the first priestess, letting her hands go and walking over to him. Once the second priestess was directly in front of Antinous, she smiled again, plucking a flower from her crown and taking Antinous' hand, pressing it into his palm.

She then leaned in and whispered something into his ear that was too low for Hadrian to hear, but Antinous' eyes widened for a moment before smiling and nodding.

The woman pulled back from Antinous' ear; then, the woman remained still while a ghostly visage of sorts continued to lean forward. The crown followed this apparition as the priestess remained still.

The ghostly woman continued to lean forward until she met Antinous' lips for a brief second and then she was gone; the two had merged once more.

Giving Antinous another smile, the Priestess let go of his hands and turned back around, making her way back to the center of the circle.

Once she reached her original spot, she joined hands with the other priestess and took a deep breath, then another, and another.

As they breathed together, the fire in the center of the room almost seemed to breathe too, ebbing and flowing with their breaths and filling the space with more and more light. It even seemed to be changing colors again, from green to pink, back to red.

At this point, the priest lowered himself to his knees and bowed, placing his forehead on the floor. He was quickly mirrored by the rest of the guests, including Hadrian himself as they made their way to the floor.

Hadrian knew that he was the emperor and he shouldn't be bowing to anyone, but something about this situation felt different. He felt almost as though he would be disappointed in himself if he didn't bow.

Everything was illuminated by the light of the fire and all the colors seemed to swirl together as if even the temple itself didn't know where it ended and where the light began.

The rest of the evening became a blur of voices and songs, embraces and dancing. At one point, the priest disappeared only to return with a fully grown bull, which he tied standing with its head over the bowl of flame.

The two priestesses watched on from their respective spots near the pedestals and once the bull was in position the first priestess opened her basket and lifted the snake off her shoulders, allowing it to curl back in on itself once more before placing it back in the basket.

The second priestess just closed the box, with her underworld crown still inside.

Once both containers were closed once more, the priest nodded and then proceeded to slit the throat of the bull, allowing the blood to fall down into the fire, extinguishing it. Eventually the bull went limp but the way it had been tied prevented it from falling onto the bowl and crushing it.

The second that the last bit of life drained from the bull's eyes, both priestesses stopped and threw their heads back. Hadrian couldn't have been sure, but it looked as though the visages that had been sharing the physical forms of the priestesses exited the temple through the oculus and then as sobering as a slap to the face, Hadrian noticed the lack of their presence.

The world seemed just a little bit less colorful and even the air surrounding them felt less alive.

Both priestesses lost their strength to stand at the same time and slumped to the ground. Immediately, the priest was checking them both and laying them down in more comfortable positions. After checking to ensure that everyone was still there and with them, he rang a bell and in came several temple servants.

It was over.

The sun shone through the oculus at the top of the temple and Hadrian looked around stunned to see the daybreak, watching as the other participants snapped back into reality with the same bewildered look on their faces that he was sure read on his own face.

He turned his head as he felt a hand rest upon his shoulder. It was Felix.

"You alright sire?"

"Yes." Hadrian nodded. "Were those?"

Felix looked up at the oculus and smiled. "Yes, I think so. It's nice to know that I didn't just make it all up as a child. They're exactly as I remember them."

In that moment, Antinous walked up to them, staring at his palm.

Hadrian and Felix watched him for a moment.

"What did she say to you?" Felix finally broke the silence.

Antinous looked up from his palm, wonder in his eyes and then looked over to Hadrian. "She said thanks for the flowers."

Hadrian felt his mouth drop open fully as Antinous revealed the palm of his hand where the priestess had pressed the ethereal flower into it. There, on the palm of his hand was something that looked sort of like a birthmark, but Hadrian knew that it hadn't been there prior to this evening.

"You've been blessed by Persephone." The priest appeared next to them, looking down at Antinous' hand thoughtfully.

"What does that mean?" Hadrian asked.

The priest shrugged. "I don't know. But should you ever find yourself in an hour of need. I would suggest going to one of her temples; it seems that she favors you and perhaps she will be able to help."

Antinous turned his attention back to the palm of his hand and ran his fingers over the new mark.

"Thank you all for participating." The priest turned to address the full room. "You are always welcome back, just remember, once you leave the doors of this temple, you may no longer speak of what you witnessed here tonight. That said, linger as long as you wish, a feast will be waiting for you when you leave. I'm sure you're all hungry."

Chapter Fourteen

"I know we aren't allowed to talk about what happened once we leave here." Antinous said, looking around the room. "But I am so hungry that I might pass out if we don't go."

Hadrian felt his own stomach growl and wondered to himself what might have been in that cup they had handed out the night before. "Me too." He agreed. "Besides, I'm not even sure I would know what to say."

"It does feel that way doesn't it?" Felix piped up, standing next to Hadrian. "Don't worry too much though, they mostly say that so details about the rite don't get out. Talking about it without actually talking about it should be fine amongst yourselves.

When I was a kid, it took me a couple of days before I had processed anything that had happened. Just don't let anyone overhear you."

"How would they know?" Antinous asked, tilting his head.

"Did you really just witness what we witnessed and believe they wouldn't?" Hadrian retorted, raising an eyebrow.

In return Antinous just blushed and shrugged sheepishly. "Fair enough."

The three of them turned to exit the temple and it seemed as though most of the other participants chose to do the same, only a few stragglers sticking back.

"So, where are we going now?" Antinous asked. "After the feast, I mean."

Hadrian pursed his lips and nodded. He would have liked to stay a little longer but with all of the tension caused by Aegeus, he knew it was best for them to move forward.

"I did have plans to tour the Peloponnese." Hadrian shrugged. "Felix and I talked about potentially heading over there at some point to do some rounds and determine what sort of needs the area has. No better time than the present I suppose."

Felix nodded curtly but added nothing more to the conversation. Turning his attention back to Antinous, he noticed that the shorter man had gone quiet. He seemed surprised by the destination and had a contemplative look about him that Hadrian didn't see on him often.

"Is that alright?" Hadrian asked as they rounded the corner into the feast hall.

"Oh, yes, why wouldn't it be?" Antinous seemed almost pulled out of a dream when Hadrian asked him, shaking his head and exerting effort to come back to the present.

They found seats and were able to sit down comfortably; the feast the other night had been particularly raucous just due to the sheer amount of people who had been present. But this feast, considering only about 10 people had been present at the greater mysteries, was considerably smaller, thus giving them more privacy to talk.

"I don't know." Hadrian took some meat from the platter in the center of the table and deposited it on his plate before going back for some fruits and veggies also placed strategically between the meats. "You just seemed to go somewhere when I mentioned where we were headed."

"It's nothing." Antinous smiled, moving some food onto his own plate. "It's just, I haven't been that far East in a while. It's close to where I grew up actually."

"Really?" Hadrian chewed thoughtfully. "I suppose it would be."

"I just haven't been back since my parents died and, I don't know, it's just weird to think about going back."

Hadrian reached over and took Antinous' hand in his own. "If it's too much, we can do something else."

Antinous shook his head and squeezed Hadrian's hand back. "No. I don't want you to have to skip an entire region because of me. I'm sure there are people living there now who need your help. Besides, it might be good for me to go back. Just because I hadn't planned on going back doesn't mean that it would be a bad thing."

Hadrian smiled and ran his free hand through Antinous' curls. "Right."

Antinous grinned and leaned forward pressing a kiss to Hadrian's lips before turning back to his food. "True. Who knows? It might even be fun. I think that all hope for my life going the way I thought it would truly went out the window the second you and I became something more serious."

Hadrian chuckled and took a drink of his wine. "Fair enough."

"Besides." Antinous continued. "As long as we are there together, it doesn't really matter where we go, does it?"

Hadrian ruffled his brows, truly touched by Antinous' sentiment. He had spent so much of his life traveling anywhere he could as long as he was nowhere near his wife that it was nice to hear the opposite. Something about traveling with Antinous and experiencing all that the world had to offer together made Hadrian feel a little bit less like he was running.

Hadrian placed his hand on Antinous' thigh under the table and smiled softly at him. "I'd go anywhere with you, I hope you know that. You make every day an adventure."

Antinous grinned and turned his attention back to his food.

Now that it was the morning, they should really be setting off, Hadrian thought. He felt as though he should be tired but when he searched himself for that feeling, it was nowhere to be found.

"We will leave after the feast." Felix, as though reading his mind, responded. "The troops should have been ready to go since last night."

"Perfect." Hadrian nodded.

"So, where to?" Felix asked, finishing off the food on his plate.

Hadrian glanced over to Antinous for a moment and then back to Felix.

"Epidaurus."

—

They rode across the landscape without much incident, it also went a little faster given they'd left an entire detachment in Athens and could maneuver considerably easier with fewer people. Even so, it still took them a couple of days to make their way to Epidaurus.

Sleeping in a tent was considerably more enjoyable now that Antinous was there to share his bed, but Hadrian still found himself missing having an actual bed. That was a feeling that he hadn't really experienced before.

"Perhaps I will begin the construction of a summer home." He mused to Antinous one night as they lay in their cot. "By the ocean, and we can stay there between trips instead of having to go back to Rome."

"Will it have a garden?" Antinous smiled, picturing it.

"Yes, of course." Hadrian replied, stroking Antinous' hair. "We can grow whatever you want and we can have an altar to Persephone if you want. We could even grow the flowers she liked so that we can change them out every day."

"I think that sounds amazing." Antinous smiled up at him, running his fingers through his beard.

Hadrian took Antinous' hand in his own and flipped it so he could look at his palm. The mark from the Mysteries was still there, just as prominent as it had been that day.

"What are you thinking?" Antinous murmured.

"Just that, I think we are very lucky to have such a powerful goddess looking down upon us with favor."

Antinous smiled. "Yes. Me too."

"It's really not necessary." Hadrian argued, shaking his head.

They had just arrived at the palace in Mantinea and already they had been swarmed with politicians insisting that they accompany them for a statue reveal the next morning.

"It really is." The man who had quickly pulled them inside said. "I insist. Besides, I understand that you wanted to see the construction progress on the Temple of Zeus, correct? We can kill two birds with one stone so to speak."

Hadrian pursed his lips and sighed. Truly he was far too tired to be having this argument right now, so against his better judgment he conceded.

"Alright. But just, no feast tonight."

The man opened his mouth as if to protest, but Hadrian held up a finger silencing him immediately.

"We have been riding for quite some time and if we are going to be at an event first thing tomorrow morning, I must insist that we use tonight to settle in and rest."

"Of course, sir." The man bowed and gestured towards a nearby door. "Here are your accommodations and please don't hesitate to reach out should you need anything at all."

"Thank you." Hadrian nodded and stalked past the man, quickly entering the space and closing the door as soon as Antinous slipped in behind him.

Hadrian sighed and made his way over to the bed, rubbing his neck.

"You seem tense." Antinous mused, following him over.

"It's nothing." Hadrian refuted. "It's just, due to the cryptic nature of the statue reveal, I'm sure it will be something in my honor and I just think that those resources could have been spent elsewhere, bettering the city."

Antinous hummed in acknowledgment and hopped up on the bed behind Hadrian, massaging his shoulders.

"It's not that I'm not grateful." Hadrian backtracked a little. "It's just... uncomfortable for me."

"Well." Antinous ran his hands down Hadrian's chest, leaning fully on his back. "I think that I can probably distract you from your stress, at least tonight."

"Mmm, you think so?" Hadrian brought his hand up to Antinous' arm and softly stroked his forearm.

"Yes," Antinous whispered into his ear. Then before he knew what was going on, Antinous had pulled away and was making his way to the space in front of Hadrian.

He smiled and climbed on top of him, straddling his lap and bringing their lips together.

"I know that we are limited in what we can do while traveling." Antinous continued between kisses. "But, tonight, we don't have any soldiers patrolling around the tent, no dirt floor to make anything uncomfortable, and a full bed to do whatever we like."

Hadrian felt a shiver go down his spine as Antinous traced a finger from his earlobe, down to his collarbone.

He wrapped his hands around the outsides of Antinous' hips and finally closed his eyes, kissing him back with a passion. He teased his tongue at Antinous' lips for a moment before he was granted access and then their tongues moved together in a practiced, sensual dance.

Hadrian could feel himself hardening with each kiss and craved more pressure. So, using his hands as leverage, he tilted Antinous' hips, grinding the other man into his lap.

Immediately understanding what he wanted, Antinous continued the movement, slowly at first, so that Hadrian could feel the drag of each movement against his slowly hardening cock. Then, he felt Antinous' length slot up against his own and he couldn't stop the growl that escaped him.

He flipped them over and pinned Antinous to the bed, now taking over the movement of hips, grinding the smaller man down into the mattress. He took a break from Antinous' mouth to kiss across his jaw and down to his neck. Biting at Antinous' pulse point gently, he felt himself twitch at the sound it pulled out of the black haired man.

So, he bit down for a second, then pulled off and latched onto Antinous' neck, sucking at the perfect skin.

Antinous' breath picked up and his hips started to move in tandem with Hadrian's. Something about being marked like this really did it for him, they had discovered, and Hadrian was more than happy to oblige. He sucked until he felt satisfied that he'd left a prominent mark before moving on to the next spot.

All the time, the grinding of their hips together was pushing him closer and closer.

"Please, fuck me..." Antinous gasped, his fingers clawing down Hadrian's clothed back.

"Well, I can't deny a request like that, can I?" Hadrian responded playfully before scooting back for a moment to remove his robe. As he took off his robe and tossed it to the floor, he watched Antinous do the same, not quite making his toss to the floor, but rather the edge of the bed, where it hung there.

Hadrian licked his lips and took Antinous by the waist, hoisting him up so he was further towards the middle of the bed before flipping him over. Antinous sat on his knees, with his face down in the mattress.

Hadrian gripped his cock, stroking it a couple of times at the sight before spreading Antinous' ass cheeks with his hands and diving in, licking a stripe right over the smaller man's hole.

Antinous howled at the contact and tried to press his hips back more, but Hadrian held him in place.

"Keep your hands above your head." Hadrian instructed.

Antinous whimpered but nodded into the sheets and arched his back.

Hadrian traced the ring of muscle with his tongue a couple of times before plunging it in. He could feel Antinous shaking with the desire to touch himself, but just as Hadrian had asked, he kept his hands together, up by his head.

Adding a finger to the mix, Hadrian pressed his index finger in, pumping it a couple of times before pulling it out and sucking at Antinous' hole again. The dual sensations had the smaller man moaning loudly into the mattress.

Leaning back again, Hadrian put his finger back inside, pumping it a couple of times before adding a second finger. He scissored them, stretching Antinous out a little before flipping his wrist and rubbing at his prostate.

Antinous panted, absolutely a mess, as he rocked his hips in time with Hadrian's movements. His cock was red and leaking, just hanging, neglected in the space between his legs. Hadrian knew that Antinous could cum with his ass alone, but that was not the goal tonight. So instead of continuing to abuse his prostate, he laid off, going back to stretching.

"Baby, baby please... fuck..." Antinous begged. Hadrian could hear his voice beginning to crack as tears gathered at the corners of his eyes.

Since spending more time with Antinous, Hadrian had learned how to play his body like an instrument. He worked him all the way up to the edge and then pulled back. Something about the way that Antinous begged made Hadrian's cock harder than anything. He had to actively resist touching himself because he could, and had cum just like this, fingering Antinous until he was in tears.

However, he didn't have enough self control to keep himself from rubbing his cock up against the shorter man's thigh every now and then just to relieve some of the pressure.

When he finally pressed a third finger in, Antinous sobbed. As he pressed his ass back, fucking himself on Hadrian's fingers, Hadrian knew exactly what he was looking for and did not give it to him, deliberately avoiding his prostate.

It was only when he simply couldn't handle it anymore that he finally pulled his fingers out and lined his cock up with Antinous' hole.

Pulling a groan out of both of them, Hadrian pushed all the way inside, draping himself over Antinous' smaller form.

"You alright?" He checked in, resisting the urge to just start thrusting immediately.

"Yes, move please." Antinous gasped.

That was all the permission Hadrian needed to pull back and thrust in again, and again. Reaching around, he took hold of Antinous' cock and stroked it to the rhythm of his thrusts. He did not let up until Antinous was begging and crying into the sheets and only when he felt Antinous clench around him, did he fall over the edge.

Chapter Fifteen

Hadrian was glad that he had insisted on taking some alone time with Antinous the night before because it truly seemed like today was just back to back events and people needing his attention. Typically, one of these days would have been awful and exhausting, but something about having Antinous there really helped him keep his head about him.

As they made their way down to the reveal, Antinous distracted him with conversation.

"So what do you think the statue is?" Antinous asked playfully.

"Oh, I don't know." Hadrian shook his head. "I try and discourage dedicating statues and non-functional monuments to me since those resources could be redirected to other things that the territory might need. Unfortunately, sometimes they slip past me before I can. I think that the worst case scenario is that it's a giant statue of me."

"I think you're the only emperor in history who has ever complained about his people dedicating a statue to his image." Antinous laughed.

Hadrian just took Antinous' hand in his own and shook his head.

When they arrived at the reveal, Hadrian closed his eyes and took a deep breath. The sheet covering the statue was huge; at least three times his size.

"Oh, they weren't kidding." Antinous said, gazing up at the figure.

"Let's get this over with." Hadrian replied through his smile.

They finally took a seat and redirected their attention to the man that had greeted them at the palace. He proudly addressed the crowd and when they had finally settled down, addressed Hadrian directly.

"Emperor, we are so grateful you have been able to come visit us right when the statue was completed, it is truly a sign from the gods that your image will continue to watch over and protect us even when you are far away."

Hadrian could see Antinous trying not to laugh from the corner of his eye. So he reached over and took Antinous by the hand, receiving a reassuring squeeze back.

"For you."

When the sheet dropped, for a moment, Hadrian was speechless. He actively put a hand to his mouth to prevent whatever noise was trying to escape from doing so.

"Is that?" Antinous began.

"Yes." Hadrian replied.

He knew that everyone was watching for his response, but he couldn't seem to determine the best sort of reaction. Because standing right there, towering over everyone, was not only a sculpture of him, but a stark naked sculpture of him.

"I think they may have underestimated you a bit." Antinous murmured, sounding a bit hysterical.

"Not the time, babe." Hadrian replied. He knew that he couldn't look over at Antinous because if he did, he would laugh and by doing so, would effectively offend everyone who brought them here and did work on this piece of... art.

So instead, Hadrian pulled from his training Trajan had insisted on all those years ago, took a deep breath, and took his hand away from his face.

"It's incredible. Thank you."

The man unveiling the statue visibly relaxed as he let out a breath.

"I'm so glad you like it." The man beamed. "Now, if you wouldn't mind accompanying us to the temple we have prepared a celebratory feast in your honor."

"The feasts never end do they?" Antinous chided, biting his lip to stifle the laughter.

"No, they don't." Hadrian shrugged, pulling Antinous in. "Not for me or for you either, now that we are together."

Antinous raised his eyebrows.

"Get ready for a lifetime of feasts and giant statues of me."

Antinous' face softened and he ran a hand across Hadrian's cheek.

"I think I can handle a lifetime of that."

— 3 YEARS LATER —

"Sir, your bags are all packed and ready to go."

Hadrian stood. It felt nice to be up and about again. After touring for another couple of years, he'd caught something and fallen ill.

Of course they'd needed to go back to Rome since traveling with his illness hadn't been a possibility. However, with Antinous by his side, he felt better about returning home, as now he had more of a reason to.

Antinous had been tireless, making himself right at home in Hadrian's bedchambers. He coordinated all the doctor appointments, the medicine that Hadrian now needed to take every day, and the levels of stress that he was exposed to daily.

"Hadrian." Antinous' voice carried through the hall as he made his way to their bedroom.

"Yes love?" Hadrian turned and held out his hands, meeting Antinous half way.

"Titus needs to know what you want inscribed on the Pantheon now that we've rebuilt it."

"Mmm." Hadrian vocalized, considering for a moment. "Just put Marcus Agrippa's information on it. He's the one who built the original."

Antinous smiled and ran his hands through Hadrian's hair. "That's what I thought you would say, so that's what I told him."

"Oh? So why did you come to ask in the first place?" Hadrian mused, pulling Antinous closer.

"Well, your wife was nearby and overheard the whole thing. I swear, she was looking at me like she wanted to castrate me when I glossed over the opportunity for you to forever inscribe your name in stone. I knew that's not what you would want though, but I did come by just to make sure we are on the same page in case she calls for my head."

"Absolutely valid." Hadrian chuckled. He leaned down and kissed Antinous softly on the lips. "Hello there."

"Hello." Antinous smiled back. "Are you sure that you're feeling up to heading out again? I wouldn't want you to push yourself to do something you weren't ready for."

Hadrian shook his head and gestured to the servants to begin moving their things outside.

"I'm sure. I'm feeling quite a bit better and the fresh air will likely do me a world of good."

Antinous pursed his lips and walked next to him, hand in hand. "Well, alright. As long as you're sure. You are no longer a spring chicken and I know that statistically I am going to outlive you but I don't need you running towards an early grave just because you want to get as far away as you can from Vibia."

Hadrian chuckled. "Oh, come now. We've talked about this. I will always make sure you're taken care of."

"That's not what I'm worried about." Antinous shot back. He stopped and pulled Hadrian into a tight hug. "You really scared me there for a while when you first got sick. I know that you would make sure I get taken care of, but I'm more worried about not having as much time with you as I can."

Hadrian buried his face in Antinous' curls and huffed. "Alright, I promise that I will be careful and not push myself to an early grave. Satisfied?"

Antinous nodded and stepped back, taking Hadrian's hand again and leading them down the hallway towards the doors. "Yes, but only because I know that I will be there to force you to see a doctor if you need it and take your meds on time. Honestly, it's a wonder how you functioned without me around for so many years."

"I wonder that sometimes too." Hadrian mused.

This time, they weren't launching a military campaign so the amount of men accompanying them was considerably less than the number they had traveled with previously.

This time, it was only Felix and a handful of additional guards.

"Are you excited to take part in the Mysteries again?" Hadrian prompted.

"Of course I am." Antinous grinned. "I am also equally excited to see the finished aqueducts you commissioned. I hope that it's been helping with the drought."

After they'd left previously, it had only taken about a week for one of Hadrian's advisors to show up and take control. Gaius was one of Hadrian's most trusted senators, he had served when Trajan was the emperor and carried over into his own rule. He had no doubt that Gaius would be able to wrangle the mess that was Aegeus, but it always brought a little joy to his heart to get updates from the senator.

A few months ago, they had received an update that the aqueducts he had commissioned when they first visited were finished. After much convincing and assurance from Antinous that there likely would not be another naked statue of him lying in wait if they showed up for the unveiling, he agreed to go.

It just so happened that the unveiling lined up with the Mysteries again and both Hadrian and Antinous had taken it as a sign from the gods that they were meant to participate again.

"Shall we?" Hadrian looked over at Felix.

Felix nodded. "Everything is ready to go. I also got word that Vibia is on her way right now to speak to you about your decision for the inscription on the Pantheon."

"Oh, I hope that you aren't going to suggest I wait for her to arrive are you?"

"Of course not." Felix huffed. "I was simply letting you know that if we leave now, the guards that I sent her way to distract her should delay her enough for us to get away."

Hadrian grinned and took Antinous by the hand. "Well then, we really should get going shouldn't we?"

Antinous laughed as they jogged over to the horses and mounted them, setting off as quickly as they could.

As they left the gates of the city, they finally slowed their pace and gave themselves an opportunity to regroup. Hadrian slowed so that his horse was trotting next to Antinous' and Felix sped up so that he was next to the two of them.

"There was one more thing." Felix said as clearly as he could without the wind taking away his words.

When Hadrian looked over, gone was the smile he'd donned at the palace. It was now replaced with something a bit more concerned.

"What's going on?" Hadrian prompted.

"There has been some unrest that has been brewing."

"Felix." Antinous shout-whispered.

Hadrian turned and saw Antinous shaking his head.

"What? What's going on?" Now incredibly concerned, Hadrian turned back to Felix.

"Antinous and I thought that it would be best to hold off on delivering this news until you were feeling better. But now that you are, you deserve to know."

Felix took a deep breath and shifted in his seat.

"There has been some talk about the nature of your relationship in some of the courts recently."

Hadrian looked over at Antinous and saw him watching the road with a sad look on his face.

"There has been talk about your relationship since you returned to Rome as I'm sure you know. Unfortunately, there has been further discussion about the appropriateness of it among the higher courts."

"The appropriateness?" Hadrian balked. "Trajan had boys and men coming and going from his chambers at all hours of the night. What could they possibly be taking issue with?"

"It's not the fact that we are both men, Hadrian." Antinous piped up. "It's the fact that I'm not just a little slave boy you bring in to fuck on the weekends."

Hadrian felt his heart drop into his stomach. "How long has this been going on?"

"Well. The gossip started nearly as soon as you returned. However, the truly concerning whispers began a few months ago."

"A few months?" Hadrian whipped his head back around to look at Antinous. "Why in the gods' green earth did you not tell me?"

"Because you were sick." Antinous furrowed his brows. "Because you didn't need to be worrying about petty gossip while you were knocking on death's door."

"I was hardly-"

"You were." Antinous interrupted. "Hadrian, you were bedridden for months."

Hadrian snapped his jaw shut.

"I can handle a few people saying things to me if-"

"I'm sorry." Hadrian interjected. "People were saying things to you? I thought this was just petty gossip."

"It was." Felix piped up. "Until a few months ago."

"Who?" Hadrian demanded.

"That's not important." Antinous protested.

"It IS important." Hadrian felt the anger bubbling up from his stomach. "I would have said something, I would have-"

"Made it worse." Antinous finished.

For a few moments it was silent. Only the sound of the horse hooves could be heard.

"All of this started because people were jealous of how much attention I got in comparison to everyone else. If I was just a slave boy that you kept on the side, at least they could look down on that person and continue pretending like they were better than them, but when we got back, you made it abundantly clear that nobody was to treat me that way. It made it difficult for them to justify you keeping me around."

"That's ridiculous." Hadrian mumbled. He was still upset, but Felix and Antinous had a good point. If he had interjected when these rumors had first surfaced despite being as sick as he was, it probably wouldn't have been a great political move and likely would have made him a considerable number of enemies.

"Was it Vibia?" Hadrian asked turning to Felix and from the look on the guard's face, he knew he was right.

"Some of the rumors and complaints that we have uncovered did originate from Vibia, yes."

Hadrian shook his head and continued forward, looking at the road. "I'm sure she doesn't actually have any feelings about my relationship with Antinous. She's likely just riding the wave in hopes of getting more people on her side. She's always been a power-hungry bitch like that."

Felix huffed. He clearly felt similarly but didn't feel it was his place to say so.

"Alright." Hadrian nodded. "So what are we going to do about all of this?"

"We're doing it." Antinous replied. "Just getting as far away from that viper as we possibly can and hoping that it sates her need for control to have us out of sight and hopefully out of mind."

Hadrian pursed his lips but said nothing, hoping with everything he had that that was true.

Chapter Sixteen

After riding for the rest of the day, they had ultimately decided to stop in a small town instead of camping. So now, as they entered their room in the inn, Hadrian closed the door softly and locked it, watching Antinous as he put his bag down and sat down on the bed.

He pursed his lips and walked over, sitting down next to the shorter man, who was trying very hard to look like he was busy with whatever piece of twine he had in his hands.

Hadrian took a breath and looked straight ahead.

"Vibia said something to you didn't she?"

Antinous' hands stuttered on the string he was messing around with for a moment but then resumed movement.

"I know that you and Felix were trying to protect me and I appreciate what you did, I do. But, now that I know, maybe you could just tell me everything and I can make up for not being able to be there for you when it happened."

Antinous pursed his lips and stared down at the string. As he blinked, one tear fell and then another, but they did not wet his face, rather falling directly into his lap.

"It's stupid." Antinous shook his head. "She cornered me after I'd gotten back from town one day. We'd never really spoken to each other, but I had seen her around so I knew who she was.

I don't know why I thought that she had anything worthwhile to say to me, but I didn't run when she called after me."

Hadrian set his jaw and continued to listen. Vibia had an awful way of saying exactly what she thought of you in a way that stuck with you. He'd been party to that conversation a couple of times and it hurt him deeply to think that Antinous had to deal with any of it.

"She basically told me that I shouldn't get too comfortable, that I was just a whore and one day you would see that and um... and leave me."

Antinous swallowed, his voice wavering.

"I told her that she didn't know what she was talking about and that if she didn't have anything else to say that I was going to leave. But, she stopped me again."

Hadrian furrowed his brows and closed his eyes.

"She said that you don't even have the capacity to love your own wife, so how could I ever possibly hope that you would love me?"

Hadrian reached over and took Antinous' hand in his own.

"I know it's not true." Antinous continued. "It was just... hurtful that she felt that way."

Hadrian turned and took Antinous' face in one hand, kissing him deeply. He felt the tears fall down Antinous' cheeks but simply wiped them away with a thumb before pulling back only so far so he could speak.

"She is hateful and jealous because I never loved her the way I love you."

Antinous sighed and turned slightly closer to Hadrian. Hadrian brought his other hand up and cupped Antinous' face between them.

"I have never loved anyone the way that I love you, Antinous."

Hadrian felt his heart break as Antinous let one sob rattle through his body.

"I will never love anyone the way I love you." Hadrian finished in a whisper.

"I love you, too." Antinous murmured. "More than anything."

Their foreheads pressed together and Hadrian could feel Antinous' breath on his lips.

"Let me worship you tonight." Hadrian whispered, dotting kisses along Antinous' neck and earlobe. "The way that I know you deserve. The way that I want to."

Hadrian traced up Antinous' neck with his nose, gently nipping behind the other man's ear. Antinous shivered and his breathing began to steady. Moving from tearful gasps to whimpering moans.

"No one will ever see me on my knees for them, Antinous, except you."

Hadrian gently pushed Antinous back on the bed and slid off onto the floor. He settled between Antinous' legs and ran his hands up the other man's thighs. When he lifted his gaze again, he saw Antinous propped up on his elbows, watching.

Hadrian smiled softly and began reaching underneath Antinous' robes, running his hands over every inch of him until he had touched his thighs, his hips, his ass, everything.

He leaned forward a little and cupped Antinous' balls with one hand, running his other over the growing bulge between his legs.

Antinous dropped his head back and his chest heaved as soft noises escaped his throat.

Hadrian massaged Antinous' length as it started to harden, making sure to twist his wrist in the way he knew the dark haired man loved and take his time. He leaned down and pressed kisses into Antinous' thighs as his hands worked and reveled in the noises of pleasure that escaped his lover's lips.

Slowly, he worked his way up until he was able to run his tongue from Antinous' balls to the base of his cock.

Antinous whimpered as he teased at the base, dragging his tongue up ever so slightly, only to return back down immediately after. He rolled Antinous' balls in his hand and blew a stream of air across his cock, relishing the shiver he received in response.

"Hadrian… please…" Antinous' words went straight to Hadrian's cock, now standing erect between his legs.

"Anything for you, my love." Hadrian wrapped his hand around the base of Antinous' cock and moved forward so that he was hovering directly over his lover's length. Gently, he licked the head, moving his tongue around the slit a couple of times before prodding at it. Antinous' hips jerked up at the contact and Hadrian felt Antinous' cock pulse.

Smiling to himself, Hadrian took the opportunity of Antinous being caught off guard to close his mouth around the head of Antinous' cock and suck.

"Ahh…" Antinous moaned. "Please baby, please, I need…"

"What do you need?" Hadrian asked. "I'll give you anything you want."

"I need… please suck my cock…"

"I am sucking your cock." Hadrian teased, closing his lips around the head one more time before giving it another suck.

"Take… take more- please… I need to feel you around me…"

Hadrian hummed, pleased that Antinous had verbalized what he wanted and leaned forward, taking more cock into his mouth.

Over the past couple of months he had gotten more practice with sucking dick, and while he couldn't take it all the way back into his throat like Antinous could, he could still get a majority of the length. So, he did.

Hadrian took Antinous' cock as far into his mouth as he could, wrapping his hand around the base length that he couldn't quite fit and got to work.

He bobbed his head, moving his hand in tandem with the movement, sucking all the way up and down and swirling his tongue at the tip when he got there.

Antinous was still on his elbows, watching with a flushed face and lustful eyes. He had his bottom lip caught between his teeth and was panting, breathing heavily through his nose.

"Fuck baby." Antinous moaned. "I love you so much, shit, you feel so good. Fuck."

Hadrian felt Antinous' thigh twitch and saw his abs start to clench and he knew that Antinous was close.

Instead of pulling off, he doubled down, sucking even harder and tightening his grip.

Antinous was an absolute mess, hips twitching upwards with each movement as he fought the desire to let his head fall back. He seemed equally as invested in watching what was going on as much as he clearly wanted to throw his head back in ecstasy.

"Baby, I'm so close... shit... I need..." Antinous begged.

Hadrian knew exactly what he needed. He knew this man's body better than he knew his own and understood every movement, every plea.

Releasing his grip on Antinous' balls he slid his now free hand downwards between Antinous' ass cheeks until he reached Antinous' hole. Taking one finger, he placed the pad of his finger up against the ring of muscle and pushed.

He didn't even slide inside, but the moment he applied that pressure, Antinous was clenching every muscle as he tipped over the edge. Hadrian swallowed preemptively as the salty cum first hit his tongue and didn't stop his movements until Antinous had gone absolutely slack underneath him. Only then did he pull off with an obscene pop and smile up at his young lover.

Antinous was laying, panting on the bed, looking absolutely spent. So, Hadrian got up off the ground and crawled up to Antinous, laying down next to him, pulling his lover in close.

Antinous curled in on him, burying his face in Hadrian's chest.

They just laid there together for some time, not saying anything and not moving from that spot.

Antinous pulled one of his hands away from his chest and moved it down Hadrian's stomach until it was cupping his hard cock.

Hadrian inhaled sharply and just held Antinous in his arms as he rubbed at his cock. It felt amazing, but was nowhere near enough to make him cum. Even so, he was content to lay here with Antinous until he decided he was ready for more.

Antinous pulled his hand up and slowly turned around so that Hadrian's front was to his back. He scooted up a little and guided Hadrian's cock between his thighs.

Hadrian wrapped his arms around Antinous and groaned deeply into his ear, pushing his hips forward. Antinous spit into his hand and used that to rub across his inner thighs and over Hadrian's cock. The spit mixed with the precum he was leaking was just enough to make things slick enough to move.

Hadrian pulled his hips back slightly before pushing them forward again, letting Antinous squeeze his cock with his muscular thighs.

Still taking things slowly, Hadrian tipped Antinous' head back and kissed him as he rocked his hips leisurely.

Hadrian claimed Antinous' mouth with his own, sliding his tongue past Antinous' bitten lips and tangling with the other man's. As they kissed, Hadrian let his hands wander all over Antinous' body. He touched him with reverence, tracing every divot, every curve of his lover's body.

Antinous was the most beautiful person Hadrian had ever laid eyes on and he was determined to shout it from the rooftops.

"You are so incredible." Hadrian whispered against Antinous' lips. He tangled his fingers through Antinous' dark curls, steadying his head so that he could not shake it in protest. Pressing their foreheads together, Hadrian continued.

"Inside and out, you are the most beautiful person I've ever known and I know in my heart that I will never love anyone the way I love you."

"Hadrian..." Antinous murmured, tears gathering in the corners of his eyes.

"You are the one person that I have met in my many years who is both so humble and so amazing. If anyone in the entire universe is worthy of being loved fully and completely. It is you."

Antinous smiled against Hadrian's mouth and took a deep breath.

"Well, Hadrian." Antinous opened his eyes and tilted his chin upwards so that he could meet Hadrian's gaze. "Show me then."

Antinous squeezed his thighs around Hadrian's still erect cock, sending a shockwave of pleasure through his body. He then leaned forward and placed his mouth directly next to Hadrian's ear, whispering.

"Make love to me."

Hadrian smiled and nodded. "Yes."

Rolling so that Antinous was on his back and Hadrian was bracing himself over him, Hadrian took his time, kissing Antinous deeply before peppering kisses across his face. He started on each cheek, lingering only for a moment before moving on to Antinous' nose, pressing a kiss to the tip. Then his forehead, his chin, below each ear, and across his jaw.

Hadrian littered kisses down Antinous' neck and across his collarbone. He was determined to kiss every inch of him.

As he made his way to Antinous' chest, he reached between the younger man's legs and began to rub at his hole.

Antinous inhaled sharply, tilting his hips down into Hadrian's touch. As he continued his assault of kisses, Hadrian pressed the pad of his finger against Antinous' hole as he had earlier, but this time, instead of stopping, he met the resistance and pressed forward, sliding his finger fully inside.

Antinous threw his head back, exposing his neck, moaning softly. Once Hadrian had made his way over Antinous' arms and legs with kisses, he rose back up, still rocking his finger inside the dark haired man and pressed an open mouthed kiss to Antinous neck.

He let his tongue trace Antinous' pulse point for a moment before sucking. He started out softly and slowly built pressure over time until Antinous was panting, rocking his hips in time with Hadrian's hand.

Then slowly, Hadrian slipped in a second finger, using the longer digit to stroke Antinous' prostate as lightly as he could manage.

Antinous was moaning loudly now, his fingers tangled up in Hadrian's hair as he was marked.

Carefully, Hadrian began scissoring his fingers, stretching out Antinous and preparing him to accommodate his girth.

As he maneuvered his fingers, he tasted a hint of metal against his tongue. Satisfied with his work, Hadrian pulled back to see a lovely, red and purple mark blooming on Antinous' skin. He smiled to himself and used his free hand to guide Antinous to his own neck.

"Mmmmmm." Antinous moaned as he sucked at Hadrian's neck. Fully immersed in marking his lover, Antinous barely even flinched as Hadrian slid in a third finger.

Satisfied that Antinous could take him now, Hadrian slowly slid his fingers out of Antinous.

Antinous let go of Hadrian's neck, groaning in protest until he realized what Hadrian was doing. He spread his legs further and Hadrian settled between them, rubbing the head of his cock against Antinous' hole.

"Hadrian." Antinous' eyes were wide as he ran his thumb over the mark he had just made on his lover's neck. "Baby, I-"

"No." Hadrian shook his head. "Don't apologize. This way, everyone will know who I belong to."

Antinous' brows drew together, touched at the sentiment. "You're the Emperor, you can hardly belong to only one person."

Hadrian cupped Antinous' face. "And yet, here I am. Belonging only to you."

Hadrian used his thumb to wipe away a stray tear that escaped from Antinous' eye before kissing him deeply.

Using one hand, Hadrian lined himself up and pushed slowly inside, pulling pleasured groans from the both of them. Shallowly thrusting, Hadrian waited a moment for them to both get accustomed to the sensation before beginning his rhythm.

He started off slowly, wanting this moment to last forever, but eventually couldn't help the speeding of his hips as he chased pleasure. Reaching between them, he took Antinous' cock in his hand and stroked him in time with his own thrusts, swallowing Antinous' moans.

"Cum with me baby." Hadrian panted against Antinous' lips.

Antinous nodded, moaning and breathing hard. It only took a couple more strokes until Antinous was clenching around him, giving Hadrian that final push to fall over the edge. Antinous' cum splashed between them as Hadrian filled him up.

Pulling Antinous close, Hadrian rolled them to the side and kissed Antinous gently.

"I love you more than anything."

Antinous smiled, running his fingers across Hadrian's cheekbones.

"I love you more than anything." Antinous replied. "Forever."

Chapter Seventeen

U pon waking the next morning, the group got back on their horses and continued their ride. This time as they arrived in Athens, they were greeted not by Aegeus, but instead by Gaius.

"Sire." Gaius bowed his head.

"Nice to see you again Gaius." Hadrian commented, hopping off his horse and walking over to his adviser. "Where is Aegeus?"

"Overseeing the final touches of the aqueducts." The corner of Gaius' mouth tilted up in a small, amused smile. "He wanted to make sure that everything was perfect for your arrival sir."

"I'm sure," Hadrian scoffed.

Gaius nodded and escorted them inside. "Things have been running fairly smoothly since you appointed me here, sire. The negative effects of the drought have been successfully mitigated and the quota imposed by the local government for olive oil production has been able to be met."

Hadrian furrowed his brow for a moment, remembering what the citizen had said to him about the quota the last time he had been here.

"It's the strangest thing." Gaius mused, catching Hadrian's attention again. "We seemed to stumble upon a misplacement of some of the oils. An inordinate amount had been going to the individuals who were facilitating the trade. I had a meeting with them about this a few months ago and we got that straightened out promptly.

I informed them that it must have been some horrible misunderstanding since if the emperor heard about a group of people taking advantage of free commerce and the success of the citizens of his empire that he would not take too kindly to it. Of course, they understood and miraculously found the missing stocks of oil, as I knew they would. Now they only take their share as they understand that the power of the emperor is backing the citizens."

Hadrian smiled. "What would I do without you, Gaius?"

"Oh, have to deal with more difficult diplomats I'm sure." Gaius didn't smile but Hadrian could hear the lilt to his voice that indicated he was amused.

"Gaius, I don't believe you've had the pleasure, but this is Antinous, my partner."

The man turned and redirected his gaze to Antinous who was now standing at Hadrian's side. Gaius' gaze flicked from the mark on Antinous' neck to the matching one on Hadrian's neck and back to Hadrian.

"It's a pleasure, Antinous." Gaius bowed his head slightly.

"Gaius has been an advisor for the emperor since when Trajan was in charge." Hadrian explained. "He was quite young when he first took up his seat, in fact he was only around your age when I was first brought to the capital but he had already been working in his position for several years."

Antinous smiled kindly at the older man. "It's a pleasure. Hadrian has had nothing but kind things to say about you."

Gaius lifted his brows, no doubt at the casual use of the emperor's name, but only nodded. "He is too kind to me."

Hadrian took Antinous' hand and followed Gaius back to their accommodations.

"Are you participating in the mysteries as well, Gaius?" Antinous piped up as they reached their quarters.

"I am not." Gaius grinned gently. "My household grew up worshiping the Roman Pantheon. As insightful as I'm sure it would be, my mother might come back from the grave to reprimand me for it and I don't believe any of us want that."

Hadrian chuckled. "Perhaps not."

Gaius nodded and turned to make his way back down the hallway when Hadrian stopped him.

"Gaius," Hadrian called out. The older man stopped and turned around, looking over his shoulder. "Thank you. For everything."

Gaius pursed his lips in an amused smile and clasped his hands behind his back. "Of course my liege."

Hadrian nodded and Gaius turned, continuing his way down the hall.

The first ceremony had been held the night prior and as Hadrian, Antinous, and Felix made their way down to the temple, they saw a wide range of faces. Some they knew from before and some that were fresh.

Felix had explained to them before they'd set out from the capital that they didn't need to go through the Lesser Mysteries again to attend the Greater Mysteries this year. He had only completed the Lesser Mysteries with them the time before so that he could accompany them throughout the entire process.

In reality, one only had to go through the Lesser Mysteries once, as once they were deemed worthy by the priests, they were always welcome at the temple.

This certainly seemed to be the case as they were greeted only with smiling faces and reverent bows as they entered the temple.

"How do they know which of us have been invited back?" Antinous asked once they were inside. "I'm sure that they can't possibly remember every single person who has completed the mysteries and been invited back. After all, you were only a child when you went through the mysteries the first time, but now as an adult you came back and they didn't so much as bat an eye."

Felix shrugged. "I don't presume to know the workings of the gods."

Hadrian hummed in understanding.

"Besides," Felix continued. "Of all the people wondering how the gods mark their faithful, are you really the one who should be questioning?"

Felix smirked as he glanced down to Antinous' hand. Embarrassed for a moment, Antinous clenched his hand into a fist and brought it up to his chest.

"Fair enough." He mumbled.

Felix and Hadrian laughed as they made their way into the temple, finally Antinous broke into a smile and chuckled along.

The priests waved them through as they continued into the center of the temple where the ceremony had taken place previously. And there, right in the center of the room, on two separate pedestals were the box and the basket.

The priests passed around the goblets, same as before and once everyone had received theirs, the doors to the center of the temple were sealed.

Hadrian brought the cup up to his lips and drank without question. The familiar taste of honey and barley caressed his tongue as the priest spoke.

"As we drink tonight, we invite the wisdom of the mysteries to open us up to the possibility through the gods."

The air in the room seemed to change as the priest tossed the rest of his drink onto the fire, eliciting the new wave of colors that reached throughout the room. When Persephone and Demeter arrived, everyone could feel it.

Demeter lifted her bronze snake out of the basket, placing it on her shoulders, and Persephone donned her crown of flowers.

As the visage of Persephone gazed around the room, she seemed to be looking for something. But the moment she laid her eyes on Antinous, she pursed her lips and a look of sadness overtook her.

Meeting eyes with Demeter, they communicated something that no one else in the room could understand only through their eyes and then just as before, Persephone turned and began walking towards them.

First, she stopped at Antinous, taking his hand and turning it over, opening up his palm. She gazed upon the mark for a moment and then brought it to her lips, kissing it as she had before. But then, she turned to Hadrian.

Hadrian had never had the full attention of the goddess on him before and it was overwhelming to say the least. He now understood why Antinous had been so out of sorts after immediately interacting with her last time.

The sensation he felt as she turned her gaze to him was unlike one he had ever experienced before. She felt cold, almost like the wind off a cliffside, but the longer he stood in her presence, the more he began to pick up on other sensations.

The feeling of sun on his face.

A stream babbling through the woods.

The smell of flowers.

She was formidable, the Queen of Hell.

But she was also comforting. The daughter of Demeter, the goddess of spring.

She leaned forward nearly touching her lips to Hadrian's ear as she had done with Antinous before, but this time she didn't say anything about flowers.

"Bring him to me."

Those words rang through Hadrian's very being to his core. He looked up and met her gaze, behind the eyes of the priestess was the unmistakable gaze of the goddess. He didn't know exactly what he was agreeing to, but there was nothing in her eyes that suggested deception. In fact, at the words, he felt an overwhelming wave of relief hit him.

He hadn't responded, but Persephone seemed to feel the shift in him at her words and she smiled softly. Then she nodded once and turned around, making her way back to the center of the circle.

Hadrian knew that the rest of the ceremony was continuing on as it had before, but he found himself almost stuck in stone, replaying that moment over and over in his mind.

"Bring him to me."

It was only when Hadrian felt a hand land on his shoulder did he snap back to the moment. Felix had come up beside him and it looked like the ceremony had been completed.

"You alright?"

Hadrian swallowed and took a deep breath. "I think so."

"What did she say?" Antinous appeared next to them and as Hadrian turned his gaze to his lover, Persephone's words washed over him once more. He felt both relief and an overwhelming amount of sadness.

He opened his mouth to tell him what she had said, but was then stopped by the feeling that perhaps he shouldn't.

"She said, thanks for the flowers." Hadrian smiled, reaching out and cupping Antinous' face.

Antinous smiled and nodded. "She thanked me last time, it's only right that she thank you this time."

In that moment, one of the priestesses called out to Antinous requesting to see the mark on his hand. As he padded over and spoke excitedly with the woman, Felix moved so he was standing right off the side of Hadrian's shoulder, slightly behind him.

"That's not what she said, is it?"

Hadrian swallowed, watching Antinous smile and laugh.

"No." Hadrian replied. "It's not."

CHAPTER EIGHTEEN

The feast in the temple was glorious. Incredible delicacies and a bounty saved only for the time where both Demeter and Persephone were walking together on earth once more.

Slowly, the sick feeling in Hadrian's gut began to subside as he enjoyed the food and company. Antinous at his side, Hadrian began to feel lighter and finally leaned into the full celebration.

As the sun began to rise, Felix gestured towards the door where a couple of palace guards were waiting.

"It looks like they are ready to show us the completed aqueduct." Felix mused.

Hadrian frowned. "I thought they were meeting us at the palace."

The three of them stood, thanked the priests and made their way out onto the street. One of the palace guards approached and bowed.

"Gaius sent us to pick you up here. He figured that you would be tired from the ceremony and feast and would benefit from a ride."

The guard gestured to a boat, floating just on the bank of the river.

"That was very thoughtful of him." Antinous smiled, reaching over and taking Hadrian's hand.

Hadrian looked over at his lover and couldn't help but smile back. "It was."

Felix nodded and they made their way over to the boat. It was a moderately sized boat that was clearly used to transport royalty to and from locations along the river.

Once they were all aboard, Hadrian and Antinous sat in the bench facing forward. Antinous pulled his feet up and laid his head on Hadrian's shoulder, snuggling in.

"I've never been on a boat like this one before," Antinous mused as they watched the bank get farther and farther away. "A neighbor of ours used to have a small fishing boat that he'd take me out on during the summer and I'd help him bring in the haul."

Hadrian smiled, pulling Antinous closer. "That sounds like fun."

"Actually, it was grueling work." Antinous laughed. "We had to put the nets out, pull them in, throw back the small fish, and bring everything back to shore. Then the real work began."

Hadrian took Antinous' face in his hands and kissed him. "Well, enjoy this ride, there will be no nets to pull in. Only relaxing."

Antinous covered one of Hadrian's hands with his own and smiled. "I love you."

"I love you, too." Hadrian replied, giving him one more kiss.

"Sir." The pair broke apart at the sound of the familiar voice and Hadrian turned his head to see Gaius emerging from the cabin.

"Oh Gaius." He grinned. "I didn't know that you were going to escort us personally. What a lovely surprise."

Gaius smiled softly and nodded. "Of course, sire. I actually have a couple of things I need your approval on before we reach our destination. It won't take more than a minute."

Gaius gestured towards the cabin and Hadrian nodded. "Of course."

He stood and turned around, kissing Antinous on the forehead. "Enjoy the ride my love, I will be right back."

Antinous nodded and turned his attention to the passing landscape.

Hadrian made eye contact with Felix and his guard nodded.

As Hadrian made his way into the cabin, he saw some pieces of parchment laid out on the desk and he made his way over.

"If you wouldn't mind." Gaius prompted, handing him a quill.

Hadrian was reaching for the quill when he heard a commotion outside. A crash followed by some shuffling.

"What was that?" Hadrian turned back towards the door.

"Nothing, I'm sure." Gaius replied. "Probably just one of the crew dropping a crate."

Hadrian nodded and began turning back to the desk when he heard the unmistakable yelp of Antinous.

"Hadrian!"

Hadrian turned on his heel immediately, dropping the quill to the ground and set off towards the door leaving Gaius sputtering behind him.

Nothing could have truly prepared him for what he saw when he exited the cabin. His eyes first searched for Antinous, finding him at the edge of the boat, being held from behind. Then, his next thought was, where is Felix?

Turning his head sharply to the right, he found him, unconscious, on the ground.

Snapping his attention back up to Antinous, he made eye contact with his lover. Antinous was steely and brave, but behind his eyes, Hadrian could see fear.

"What is going on here?" Hadrian boomed.

Just then, Gaius returned to the deck, sighing as he exited the cabin. "You were supposed to do this quietly."

Hadrian felt rage bubbling in his stomach as he whipped his head over to Gaius. "You attack my lieutenant and now you have Antinous over there being held hostage. I DEMAND to know what is going on, now."

Hadrian watched Gaius' face go from calm, to irritated, to exasperated.

"It is not my fault that this one is so loud." Hadrian turned his attention back to Antinous as the man holding him spoke.

The longer he looked, the more he was convinced he knew him, until the light finally hit his face.

"Aegeus." Hadrian spat. "What the fuck do you think you're doing?"

"This brat thinks he's better than everyone else." Aegeus replied venomously, tightening his grip. "And you allow it!"

"Silence, Aegeus," Gaius spoke with authority.

Gaius walked over to Hadrian and turned so they were facing each other.

"The nature of your relationship is inappropriate, my liege. Believe me when I say this is for the best."

Hadrian's eyes widened in shock. "What is for the best?"

"Hold him back," Gaius commanded, and some of the guards suddenly appeared beside Hadrian, holding his arms so he couldn't move.

"Let me go!" Hadrian demanded, struggling against the strength of the guards. He wasn't a weak man, but at his age, his strength wasn't what it used to be and he was unable to budge against the three guards holding him.

"Hadrian!" Antinous shouted again as Aegeus moved them both closer to the edge of the boat.

"Antinous!" Hadrian yelled, fighting against his captors.

"Sire. Please." Gaius tried, but Hadrian was hearing none of it.

He struggled and shouted, the full gravity of the situation dawning on him. Felix was unconscious and they were on a boat in the middle of the river. Even if someone were to hear him, they wouldn't be able to get to him in time.

"Aegeus, please!" Hadrian begged. "Let him go. I will give you... anything you want."

Aegeus stopped and met Hadrian's gaze. He smiled cruelly and tightened his grip on Antinous.

"Sorry. That ship has sailed."

Hadrian felt his stomach drop as Aegeus gave one last laugh and jumped backwards off the boat.

"ANTINOUS!" Hadrian screamed, reaching out as the love of his life was dragged backwards, off the boat and into the water.

Hadrian fought against the grip of the guards as hard as he could, wrenching himself in every direction and even using his full body weight to throw the guards off balance.

"Please! Let me go! Let me help him! ANTINOUS!"

"What are you going to do sire?" The cold tone of Gaius' voice cut through. "Jump in after him? You've been ill, your constitution wouldn't be able to take it."

"I don't care!" Hadrian spat. "Let me go NOW!"

How long had they been underwater at this point? He couldn't tell... everything was moving both far too quickly and at a snail pace. Someone needed to help, Hadrian thought as his blood ran cold.

"That's the problem, sire." Gaius shook his head, moving into Hadrian's range of vision. "You are putting his life before your own. You are the emperor, he is just-"

"Just nothing." Hadrian interrupted, his breathing becoming panicked. "He is the love of my life Gaius, please, let me rescue him!"

Hadrian felt his heart pounding in his chest as Gaius, his trusted advisor stared down at him.

"No."

Hadrian was about to scream back when he heard the surprised "oof" of a guard and another splash.

He whipped his head around to see what had happened, but saw nothing. Except...

Felix was gone.

A wisp of hope bloomed in his chest; Felix had jumped in after Antinous, he would rescue him.

"Felix will rescue him." He said out loud and watched in pleasure as Gaius realized what had happened.

"I thought I told you to incapacitate him!" He shouted at the guards next to where Felix's body had been.

"We did." One guard with a bloody nose said. "We didn't think we needed to tie him up."

Hadrian's gaze moved back to Gaius and he stared him down with a steely calm.

"You would do well to order your guards to stand down. Now that Felix is awake and he is saving Antinous, they are outmatched."

Gaius watched angrily as Hadrian spoke.

"You, will be punished for your crimes, but these guards who were just following orders; might be spared if they let. Me. Go. Right now."

He felt the doubt spread through the guards like a wave and at the first sign of them letting go, he wrenched himself free. Storming forward, he grabbed Gaius by the front of his robes.

"You disgust me." He spat.

"Sire." A guard from the front of the boat called and Hadrian turned his attention to see Felix climbing back on board, Antinous in tow.

With all his strength he threw Gaius down to the side, paying no mind to the sickening crack that sounded as he landed. Running as fast as he could, Hadrian made his way to the front of the boat, pulling Felix over the side and onto the deck.

Felix was panting and coughing as he rolled Antinous onto his back.

"Thank you, thank you, Felix." Hadrian felt tears gathering in the corners of his eyes.

"Don't thank me yet." Felix got out. "I don't think he's breathing."

For the second time, Hadrian felt his blood run cold. He turned his full attention to Antinous who was laying on the deck.

He pressed his ear to Antinous' chest, desperate to hear something, anything. But was met with nothing.

"Please." He whispered, cupping Antinous' face and kissing him over and over. "Baby please, come back to me."

Hadrian watched, hoping and praying to everything he knew to hope and pray that Antinous would wake up. But all he was met with was Antinous' still face, eyes closed.

"Please!" Hadrian wailed. The tears began welling up in his eyes as he shook Antinous by the shoulders. "Please, I can't do this without you."

The boat was silent as he shook his head, kneeling next to his lover.

When the tears started to fall, he didn't even register they were his own. All he knew was that he couldn't see as well anymore and that more water was falling onto Antinous' beautiful face.

Hadrian stroked Antinous' face over and over again, pushing the hair from his forehead and running his fingers through his locks.

"Please." He whispered again, resting his head on Antinous' chest; desperate for a heartbeat, a breath, anything at all. But was met only with silence.

"I love you." He murmured into Antinous' chest, clutching at his robes. "Please don't leave me."

He closed his eyes and held tight, unwilling to acknowledge anything else. He couldn't move, couldn't breathe until Antinous was back with him.

"Sire." Felix's voice broke through his haze and he lifted his head to see the other man leaning down on the other side of Antinous' body. "He's..."

"Don't." Hadrian begged, feeling a fresh wave of tears fall down his cheeks. "Please."

Felix watched him, tears gathering in his eyes as well. "Hadrian."

Never in the years they had spent together had Felix ever referred to him that way.

Hadrian shook his head. "Please, he can't be."

"I'm so sorry." Felix replied, his voice breaking. "I told you I'd protect him."

Hadrian shut his eyes and lowered his head back down to rest on Antinous' still chest.

"Bring him to me."

Opening his eyes in a flash, Hadrian remembered Persephone's words like they were being spoken to him now.

He sat up and turned to face the guards. "Turn this boat around."

CHAPTER NINETEEN

Hadrian held Antinous in his arms as they disembarked the boat, Felix on his heels. He'd instructed the guards on the land to watch the men on the boat and not let anyone leave or speak under threat of execution and then set off towards the temple.

"What is it, Hadrian?" Felix asked, tailing his steps.

"Bring him to me." Hadrian repeated.

"What?"

"That's what she said to me. Bring him to me." Hadrian kept walking as quickly as he could, holding Antinous' waterlogged body.

Felix said nothing more but followed in silence.

When they entered the temple, Hadrian was met by one of the priests that had been in attendance at the Greater Mysteries the night before.

"I need to speak to Persephone." Hadrian spoke clearly and with as much authority as he could. He had no idea if the priests had been expecting him or not but all he received was a nod and the priests led them to the center of the temple where the mysteries had been held.

Hadrian walked right in, but the priests stopped Felix at the door.

"I'll be right outside." Felix assured him. Then the doors were closed and he was alone.

"Persephone." Hadrian called tentatively, stumbling into the center of the room.

The dust from the fire ashes were floating in the light of the oculus but other than that, there was no movement.

"Please." Hadrian shook his head, moving to his knees and laying Antinous down on the floor. "You told me... you told me to bring him to you." Hadrian pushed through the choking feeling, stopping his voice from working properly as he began to sob again. "This is what you meant."

Hadrian looked around the temple, which remained still.

"Right?"

His voice echoed in the chamber. Biting his lip, he looked down at Antinous' face.

If he didn't know any better, he would think that he was just sleeping. He'd seen this peaceful face on his lover many times, before he fell asleep at night and just as he woke up in the morning.

Hadrian took Antinous' hand and pressed the palm to his lips, kissing it before holding it to his face as if Antinous were comforting him. He shut his eyes and began to cry, he wailed, letting out everything he had on the boat and more.

"Please." He begged again. "I can't... I can't do this without him."

As he spoke, he felt the air shift ever so slightly. But he wouldn't have opened his eyes again if he hadn't heard it.

"I'm so sorry."

Opening his eyes, he looked up and saw her. Less corporeal than she had been inhabiting the body of the priestess but still visible.

"You knew this was going to happen." Hadrian spoke. It wasn't accusatory, nor was it a question.

"Yes."

"That's why you looked so sad last night."

"Yes."

Hadrian continued holding Antinous' hand to his face, not moving.

"Bring him back. Please."

Persephone pursed her lips into a fine line and she moved across the floor silently, as if she were floating.

Once she reached them, she knelt down and placed a hand on Antinous' chest.

"I can't."

With those words, Hadrian felt the last bit of hope he was holding on to shatter in his chest.

"Then take me to him." Hadrian sighed. "Let me go to where he is."

Persephone shook her head and smiled sadly. "It is not your time yet."

"It wasn't his time either." Hadrian shot back, lip trembling. "How, how is it fair? I should have gone first."

"It was his time." Persephone replied. "But no one ever said it was fair."

Hadrian looked down at Antinous, tears streaming down his face.

"Why then?" He practically whispered. "Why have me bring him here? If you can't..."

Persephone sighed and reached out, placing her hand on the other side of Hadrian's face.

"I can't bring him back... but, there is something I can do."

Hadrian looked up and met her gaze.

"Your love, and dedication..." She began. "It has given us one more option."

Hadrian waited in silence for her to continue.

"I can make him like me." She confessed. "That way, while he won't be with you physically, he will always be with you and will be waiting for you when it's your time."

Hadrian furrowed his brows, a few more tears sliding down his cheeks. "How long will that be?"

"Ten years."

"Ten years." Hadrian scoffed. He shook his head and ran his fingers through Antinous' hair.

"I promise, Hadrian." Persephone murmured. "I will watch after him. Just, go home, build him an altar, and pray every night. He will be there."

"And then we can be together again?"

"Forever." Persephone promised.

Hadrian nodded and gently placed Antinous' hand on his chest.

"Can he hear me now?" He asked.

"Yes."

"Antinous." Hadrian's voice broke. "Baby. I love you more than anything and I always will. You changed my life in ways I never thought possible and I will never forget that."

He didn't even try to hold back the tears that flowed.

"Please wait for me. I will never forget you; I will pray every night. Just please stay by my side. I will be counting down the years until we can be together again."

Then he leaned forward and pressed one final kiss to Antinous' lips and then his forehead.

"I love you, too." The voice was so quiet, Hadrian almost didn't catch it. But he did.

Looking up at Persephone he steadied himself. "What now?"

"You continue on." Persephone replied. "I will take care of him, I swear."

Hadrian nodded and stood up, taking one final look at Antinous' body.

"Why?" The question escaped his lips before he could consider anything else.

Persephone, to her credit, seemed to know exactly what he was asking.

"The flowers."

"The flowers?" Hadrian repeated back lifting his eyes to meet Persephone's.

"He left me flowers, but he also left some for my husband."

Hadrian thought back to that day at the stall.

"Because I know she's coming back to be with her mother, but I always wondered if she missed Hades while she was away. So, if we had something darker, it might remind her of home and help the transition feel easier."

"I do miss him." Persephone admitted. "Every day."

"But you always go back to him." Hadrian replied and Persephone nodded.

"Always."

Hadrian nodded and turned, walking to the doors of the temple. Before leaving he turned around and looked back one last time; just in time to see Persephone lean down and take Antinous in her arms.

Then together, they both disappeared.

"Where is Antinous' body?" Felix asked as Hadrian walked out the doors.

"With Persephone." He replied.

Felix nodded and sighed.

The tears had stopped flowing and Hadrian was just left with a profound feeling of emptiness.

He moved to walk and Felix was immediately next to him.

"Where is Gaius?"

"Still on the boat sire."

"And Aegeus?"

"Dead."

"You're sure?"

Felix set his lips in a thin line and nodded curtly. "Slit his throat myself. He should be rotting at the bottom of the river by now."

Hadrian nodded and continued forward.

When they reached the docks, everyone sprung to attention and stood quietly. Hadrian and Felix climbed onto the boat and walked over to Gaius, who was sitting on the floor of the deck, holding his arm.

Slowly he got up and stood facing Hadrian.

"Is the boy dead?"

Hadrian tightened his jaw and stared at the other man in silence.

"Come now sire, it was for the best." Gaius continued. "Trajan wouldn't have approved of your relationship being as intimate as it was. You already have a wife. If it makes you feel better, we can find you another boy to f-"

Gaius was cut off as Hadrian lifted his hand and punched the older man in the jaw with as much might as he could muster, sending him to the floor again.

Gaius groaned in pain, holding his face as he bled from the mouth.

Hadrian turned to the nearest guards. "Bring him back to the palace, remove his tongue, and throw him in the prison."

Gaius looked up at him with shock.

"He doesn't deserve to ever speak again." Hadrian looked down on him, spitting in his general direction. He then turned to the rest of the guards on the boat.

"The two conspirators that led to the death of Antinous are being dealt with. Aegeus is dead at the bottom of the river and Gaius will spend the rest of his life as a prisoner, unable to speak. Anyone else who speaks ill of Antinous will receive the same fate. Do I make myself clear?"

For a moment no one spoke.

"I said, DO I MAKE MYSELF CLEAR?" Hadrian shouted and was immediately met with a resounding chorus of voices.

"Good." Hadrian turned to Felix. "Send word back to the capital of what has occurred today along with the new edict. Anyone who dares to speak of

Antinous or our relationship in a negative light will be punished and that includes, wives of the Emperor."

Felix nodded.

"Then, send word to all the artists we know. Everyone is to create a piece in the image of Antinous. He has been deified now and is to be treated with the respect any deity deserves."

"Yes sire."

Hadrian turned and looked at Gaius one more time in disgust before turning on his heel and walking off the boat.

He didn't need to look behind him to know that Felix was following.

The moment they were out of sight of the boat however, Hadrian stumbled over to the nearest bench and sat down, burying his face in his hands.

He felt Felix sit down next to him but neither said a word.

They sat in silence for a long time before Hadrian finally broke it.

"Ten years." He shook his head, looking out across the garden. "How am I supposed to go on without him for ten years?"

Felix pursed his lips in consideration and shrugged. "You don't."

Hadrian glanced up at his guard.

"You won't have to. If he's with Persephone, then that means he's always with you."

Hadrian laughed sadly. "Yes, I know. It's just…"

"Not the same?" Felix finished.

"Exactly." Hadrian nodded. "It's not the same."

Hadrian clasped his hands together. "I miss his warmth already."

Felix sat silently in consideration for a moment before standing.

"Come on."

Hadrian looked up in confusion. "What?"

"Come with me." Felix took Hadrian by the wrist and stood him up, walking with purpose through the garden and out onto the street.

Hadrian was in the dark about what was going on until they stopped at a flower booth. The same flower booth in fact that he and Antinous had bought flowers for Demeter, Persephone, and Hades all that time ago.

"What can I get for you?" The man asked.

Hadrian scanned the flowers for a moment before landing on some roses in the back row. "Those please."

"Excellent choice sir, how many?" The vendor prompted.

"All of them." Hadrian replied, smiling softly at the shocked face of the flower man. "I would like to purchase as many as you have."

—

Back at the palace, Felix had left him at the master bedroom.

Now that Aegeus was gone and so was Gaius, there was nobody inhabiting this area of the palace.

Felix had thought he might be more comfortable in the room that he'd stayed in when they had first arrived here, but Hadrian had refused. The memory of Antinous was still too painful to stay in a place where they had been together.

Two wagons full of roses had accompanied them back from the marketplace and Hadrian had had them delivered directly to his room.

Looking around, he scoped out the best space to set up the altar and ended up deciding on a shelf in the wall across from the bed. Carefully he removed the vases that currently inhabited that area, placing them to the side and then got to work setting up the altar.

With each rose he placed, he thought of Antinous.

His smile.

His eyes.

His laugh.

Every single thing about him, until he was done.

Then, finally stepping back, he took a moment to appreciate it. It almost looked as though the roses were exploding out of the wall, looking more like a living creation than an altar. But, something about that felt right.

"I love you Antinous. Always will." Hadrian whispered to the roses, and while he didn't hear anything back, he felt it, Antinous' love, all around him.

CHAPTER TWENTY

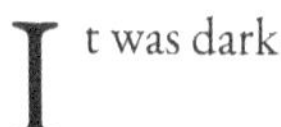t was dark.

Fuck.

Why was it dark?

What was happening?

Antinous couldn't really open his eyes. Or were his eyes already open? Was there just nothing to see?

He had been on a boat... and then...

He couldn't quite remember.

"Antinous."

Antinous turned his head towards the source of the noise. It was a woman's voice. Familiar... somehow.

But he still couldn't see. If only he could…

Then suddenly there was a light in the dark and in the center of that light was a face he would recognize anywhere.

It was Hadrian.

But why was he crying? And who was that on the ground at his knees?

He looked familiar…

"Antinous."

From behind him the woman's voice called out once more. This time he recognized it.

"Mother?"

Only silence and darkness met him in response. He could hear the waves of water crashing upon a bank. Aside from that there was a tinkling of coins and nothing else.

Turning back, he saw that Hadrian was farther away, as if looking back had moved him physically. So he took one step and then another.

"Antinous."

This time when the woman's voice called out, he ignored it. He had known who it was, but now he did not. It almost seemed like the further he got away from the sounds of the river and the coins, the less he could remember about the voice.

But there, in front of him, bathed in a glorious golden light, was Hadrian.

So he didn't stop, he kept moving forward until he was closer and closer and he was right there!

Then suddenly, he was in the temple.

The darkness behind him was gone and he was surrounded now by the stone walls of the temple where they had just completed the Greater Mysteries.

"Welcome." A different female voice rang in his ears, this one seemed much closer.

Antinous turned to his right and saw a beautiful woman in a flower crown. Her hair shifted with the light so he couldn't quite put a color to it and her gown seemed both to float above the ground and meld with it at the same time.

"Why..." Antinous began, but he stopped as the woman put a finger to her lips and gestured back over to Hadrian.

"Please." He called into the empty temple space. "You told me... you told me to bring him to you."

Antinous stepped forward slightly and peered over at his love, then at the man lying at his knees.

"This is what you meant. Right?"

Antinous squinted at the face of the man and furrowed his brow. It was like the knowledge he was looking for was right there, but he couldn't quite reach it.

So he took one more step and then he saw it.

That was his face.

And it all came rushing back.

Aegeus, the boat, drowning...

"I'm dead." As he spoke it almost seemed comical. There he was, lying on the floor of the temple, but he was still here. Watching it all unfold.

"Yes. You are." Antinous startled slightly as he had forgotten that the woman was there for a moment.

"I..." Antinous stuttered, looking back and forth between his body and the woman.

She approached slowly before reaching out and taking his hand. The feeling was warm, comforting, familiar...

"You're Persephone." Antinous felt his eyes widen.

Persephone smiled and lifted his hand, turning the palm right side up so she could look at the mark she had placed there during his first experience here.

"Yes." Persephone looked up and met his gaze again. "I am."

"I have so many questions." Antinous shook his head, looking back at Hadrian and his body in the middle of the temple. They seemed almost frozen in time.

"I know you do." Persephone nodded, letting go of his hand. "Unfortunately we don't have time right now for me to explain everything. I need a decision from you."

"A decision?" Antinous turned back to Persephone, more confused than ever.

"Yes." Persephone walked up to him and placed a hand on his shoulder, turning him so that they were both facing Hadrian. "You died in the river, as I'm sure you remember, but I'm here to offer you a choice."

Persephone lifted her chin.

"I knew the moment I touched you what your fate was, and after feeling your love and devotion for this man and his to you, I knew it wasn't fair."

Persephone glanced over at Hadrian, who was now holding Antinous' hand up to his face and kissing it.

Antinous could almost feel his touch.

"So, I can't bring you back. But I can make it so you can stay with him."

Antinous snapped his head back to Persephone and set his jaw.

"Yes."

Persephone lifted her brow. "I haven't even explained to you how yet or what your other option is."

"I don't care." Antinous shook his head. "I want to stay with him."

Antinous watched as Persephone's face softened and she smiled. "I knew I made the right choice."

Persephone walked over to where Hadrian was kneeling. "There's only one last thing I need to make this a viable option."

Antinous watched as her form shimmered slightly and became slightly sharper. He then watched in awe as Hadrian focused his gaze on her, clearly seeing her as well.

"I'm so sorry." She murmured.

"You knew this was going to happen."

"Yes."

"That's why you looked so sad last night."

"Yes."

Antinous felt his heart break in his chest as he watched Hadrian sob, clutching his body.

"Bring him back. Please."

He watched as Persephone placed a hand on his body and shook her head.

"I can't."

"Then take me to him." Antinous stepped forward, almost crying out that he couldn't possibly, but he found that he had no voice to speak.

"Let me go to where he is."

Luckily, Persephone got to it first.

"It is not your time yet."

"It wasn't his time either."

Antinous clutched his chest, feeling tears begin to fall. "Oh Hadrian."

"How, how is it fair? I should have gone first."

"It was his time." Persephone replied. "But no one ever said it was fair."

As Hadrian looked down at his body, Antinous stepped forward into the light, right behind Persephone.

"Why then? Why have me bring him here? If you can't..."

Antinous felt his heart crying out as he watched Persephone cradle Hadrian's face. He wanted to be the one comforting him, but he knew that he couldn't. At least not right now.

"I can't bring him back... but, there is something I can do. Your love, and dedication..." She began. "It has given us one more option."

Antinous shifted on his feet, waiting for her to continue.

"I can make him like me."

Antinous felt his mouth drop open. Him? A god? That had to be some sort of cosmic joke.

"That way, while he won't be with you physically, he will always be with you and will be waiting for you when it's your time."

"How long will that be?" As Hadrian asked, Antinous found himself hanging on every word.

"Ten years."

"Ten years?" Antinous blurted out. "That's... such a long time..."

"I promise, Hadrian." Persephone murmured. "I will watch after him. Just, go home, build him an altar, and pray every night. He will be there."

"I will?" Asked Antinous, watching Persephone speak to Hadrian.

"And then we can be together again?"

"Forever." Persephone promised.

Hadrian nodded and gently placed Antinous' hand on his chest.

"Can he hear me now?" Antinous bit his lip, feeling the tears start to build again.

"Yes, baby. I can hear you." He whispered, knowing very well that Hadrian couldn't hear him back.

"Yes."

"Antinous. Baby. I love you more than anything and I always will. You changed my life in ways I never thought possible and I will never forget that."

Antinous knelt down next to his lover, and let a full sob wrack his body. He was so close, but he couldn't reach out and touch him. He couldn't kiss him. He couldn't...

"Please wait for me. I will never forget you; I will pray every night. Just please stay by my side. I will be counting down the years until we can be together again."

Then he leaned forward and pressed one final kiss to Antinous' lips and then his forehead and as he did. Antinous, against all odds, felt the pressure.

"I love you, too." He spoke.

He didn't know if Hadrian had heard him but he felt like he needed to say it anyway.

Hadrian looked up at Persephone again. "What now?"

"You continue on." Persephone replied. "I will take care of him, I swear."

Just before Hadrian left the room, he paused. "Why?"

Persephone just smiled. "The flowers."

Antinous was confused for a moment, but then he remembered. That day at the market, he had insisted that they get some flowers to honor Hades so that she could remember him while she was away and suddenly it clicked.

"He left me flowers, but he also left some for my husband."

Persephone was doing this for him because of what he did for her.

"I do miss him." Persephone admitted. "Every day."

"But you always go back to him." Hadrian nodded.

"Always." Persephone replied.

Antinous felt his heart being torn in two as he watched Hadrian walk away. But he kept silent, ready to hear what Persephone had to say about how all this would work.

Persephone took his body in her arms and shimmered back into the form he had seen her in previously. His body was gone but in her hands was an amulet.

"Do we have time for questions now?" Antinous asked, breaking the silence.

Persephone laughed. "Yes, we do."

Antinous sighed and sat down on the floor of the temple not even a little bit sure where to start.

"So, am I a god now?"

"Yes, in theory." Persephone replied, settling on the floor next to him.

"In theory?"

"Hadrian still has to do his part." She explained. "Gods are only gods as long as there is someone out there who worships them."

Antinous watched her in silence, waiting for her to continue.

"Until he makes your altar, you can only roam freely here within the temple. But once he makes that space, you will be able to move to the altar."

She reached out and placed the amulet in his hand, closing his fingers around it.

"This is the most important part." She pulled her hands away. "Once he makes the altar, place this amulet on the altar for him to find. As long as he wears it, you will be able to go where he goes. It acts as a portable altar of sorts."

"So..." Antinous clutched the amulet tightly. "I can only go where altars dedicated to me are?"

"Well." Persephone shrugged. "There are ranges and a lot of other things that you'll probably figure out the longer that you're worshiped. But those are things that you'll need to find out for yourself. The important part is that you don't have to leave his side."

Antinous blinked at the amulet. "Thank you." He murmured.

Persephone smiled. "If you ever want to talk, just find an altar of mine and... watch over him, alright?"

"I will." Antinous smiled, tears rolling down his cheeks. "Thank you so much."

Somewhere in the back of his mind, Antinous felt the pull of something across town. "What..."

"He's already getting started, I see." Persephone smiled softly. "Once that connection feels less like a pull and more like a pathway, that means that the altar is complete."

Persephone got up off the floor and Antinous followed.

"I mean it, Antinous." Persephone reached out and placed a hand on his arm. "If you ever need anything."

Antinous smiled. "I will. Thank you."

With that, Persephone turned around and made her way out of the temple, disappearing the moment she exited the doors.

Turns out Persephone had been right when she'd said that there were a lot of things that he needed to figure out on his own.

The night Hadrian had finished his altar, Antinous had immediately gone to visit and then gotten horribly emotional at how beautiful it all was. He found a place to put the amulet on the altar, but unfortunately, it was so filled with roses that Hadrian didn't see it at first. So after a day or so of him missing it completely, Antinous stretched to the farthest he could away from the altar space and placed the amulet on his pillow. The one next to Hadrian where he would have slept were he still alive.

The next morning, Hadrian saw it and as he took it in his hands suddenly Antinous felt unrestrained and he ran right to him.

He threw his arms around Hadrian and though he knew that Hadrian couldn't really feel it, it felt so amazing to hold him again that he didn't care.

"Antinous?" Hadrian spoke to the room.

"Yes?" Antinous replied. "Baby? I'm right here."

Hadrian put the amulet on and walked over to the altar.

"If you're here, and you can hear me, baby please give me a sign." Hadrian asked, tearing up again.

Antinous looked around the room for something to do, but ultimately picked a flower and placed it on Hadrian's pillow. Then with all his might, he willed Hadrian to turn around.

When he did, Antinous had to physically hold himself to prevent himself from falling apart with joy as tears spilled over Hadrian's cheeks and he picked up the rose.

"Baby." Hadrian's voice broke. "I knew it, I knew you'd never leave me."

Antinous just smiled and finally relaxed.

Ten years was a long time, but in the grand scheme of things, Antinous supposed that it wasn't really that bad. Besides he could be with Hadrian every moment of every day if he wanted to; and he was for a while, but eventually he decided to start testing some of his godly abilities.

For example, figuring out how the whole altar thing worked.

Turns out that there was a range of how far he could go away from the center of the altar, however, the more dedicated the believers of the altar, the further he could go.

This made it difficult in the first couple of years to find one of Persephone's temples as it seemed that they were always just out of reach.

However, due to Hadrian's insistence that many statues and paintings of Antinous be created, Antinous' popularity grew. As his popularity grew, so did Antinous' god power, which allowed him to reach out further into the world.

It was nice, having a friend and they still talked from time to time.

With Hadrian being his most dedicated supporter, of course, he found that he could roam the furthest around the amulet.

When Hadrian returned to Rome, Antinous made sure to spend some extra time making things difficult for Vibia. Nothing too drastic, not that he could do much in the way of interacting with the corporeal world, but just certain things that made her day to day difficult.

When Hadrian got wind of it, he had just chuckled and said something under his breath about "that's what you get when you send an assassin to kill my partner".

Antinous had then pushed a vase off of a shelf, effectively spooking every guard in the vicinity.

He'd been particularly proud of that one.

It wasn't all good though, he missed Hadrian. He knew that he was right there, but they couldn't really interact and he had to sit, unable to do anything when he would get sad, miss him, or get sick. There was nothing more Antinous wanted more desperately than to run his hand across Hadrian's cheek.

He was very proud however of how Hadrian kept up with everything.

He watched as he inaugurated his new Panhellenion and visited Jerusalem. Doing what he did best.

He watched as Hadrian set up the plan for his succession and watched as he retired to the countryside, in that beautiful villa with a rose garden, just like he'd always promised.

And he was there.

Until the very end.

Chapter Twenty-One

Hadrian sat in his chair, rocking back and forth as he gazed out the window at the garden.

"You would have really enjoyed living here, Antinous," Hadrian spoke, rubbing the amulet between his fingers. "I designed it especially so that every window looks out to the garden so that we never forget to prune the flowers."

His ten years had passed and now he waited.

His health had continued to fail, but he had never let that stop him from doing everything he could to create lasting good. He just thought about what Antinous would have wanted.

He knew his time was coming, but he wasn't afraid. In fact, he felt a little giddy.

Persephone had told him that they would be together again and while he'd never had the opportunity to speak to her since that day, he never gave up hope.

There were little things every day that reminded him to keep going, until the day they could be together again.

A rose on his pillow every now and then, a misfortune on his late wife, or even an overwhelming feeling of comfort. He knew Antinous was with him, he just couldn't wait until they were together again.

Looking back on his life, he had tried to do as much good as he could.

For the first time in many years, he allowed himself to consider the question that had often kept him up at night before Antinous had come along.

What will I be remembered for?

Will I be remembered for my great deeds or grand failures?

Will I be remembered as a good man?

I hope so.

Hadrian closed his eyes as he felt his breathing begin to slow.

It was close now.

He could almost feel Antinous' embrace around him as he smelled the roses.

And then...

Nothing.

"Hadrian!"

Hadrian snapped his eyes open again and found himself standing in the center of the room.

And right there.

At the door.

Was...

"Antinous!"

Hadrian broke into a run, meeting Antinous halfway and scooping him up in his arms.

"Baby! I've waited so long! I missed you." Antinous sobbed, burying his face in Hadrian's neck.

Hadrian felt tears rolling down his face as well but all he could feel was complete and utter joy.

He ran his hands through Antinous' beautiful curly hair and cupped his face.

"I missed you, so much." Hadrian murmured, bringing their lips together.

And as they kissed, it was like nothing had changed.

Hadrian kissed him with everything he had kept inside over the years. He put everything into that kiss; every I love you, every I miss you, and every I wish you were with me.

He pulled back just enough to touch their foreheads together in the embrace.

"It worked." Antinous grinned. "Just like she said."

"I think we owe a very great deal to Persephone." Hadrian chuckled, reveling in the feeling of Antinous in his arms again.

Antinous laughed through the tears and breathed in Hadrian's scent. "I can finally smell you again."

Hadrian took a deep breath and sure enough, there it was, Antinous' distinct smell that he'd been missing for nearly ten years.

"It smells like home." Hadrian whispered.

Antinous grinned up at him and ran a hand down his cheek. "I love you, Hadrian."

"I love you, too." Hadrian smiled, leaning back down and claiming Antinous' lips with his own once more.

"Come on," Antinous said excitedly. "We need to go find Persephone and officially introduce you two!"

"In a minute." Hadrian smiled, pulling Antinous even closer. "I want as much time with you as I can get first."

"Well, we do have quite a bit of that." Antinous teased, kissing the tip of Hadrian's nose.

"An eternity?" Hadrian asked, smiling ear to ear.

"That about sums it up." Antinous replied. "Forever and ever, baby."

BOOKS BY HARLOWE SAVAGE

The Monarchs of Eros Series

Alexander

Emperor Ai

Hadrian

ABOUT AUTHOR

Harlowe Savage is a queer author dedicated to creating stories that depict queer romances with the same amount of spice and passion that readers get from their straight counterparts. She firmly believes that the gap between the amount of LGBTQIA+ erotica and heterosexual erotica in the mainstream is far too large and intends to rectify this through normalizing queer romance novels and increasing accessibility of the genre.

www.harlowesavage.com

instagram.com/harlowesavage/

tiktok.com/@harlowesavage